W9-BVJ-236

Ralph Compton:
Death of a Hangman

This Large Print Book carries the
Seal of Approval of N.A.V.H.

A RALPH COMPTON NOVEL

RALPH COMPTON: DEATH OF A HANGMAN

JOSEPH A. WEST

THORNDIKE PRESS
A part of Gale, Cengage Learning

GALE
CENGAGE Learning

Detroit • New York • San Francisco • New Haven, Conn • Waterville, Maine • London

GALE
CENGAGE Learning

LIBRARY OF CONGRESS CATALOGING-IN-PUBLICATION DATA

West, Joseph A.
 [Death of a hangman]
 Ralph Compton, Death of a hangman : a Ralph Compton novel / by Joseph A. West.
  p. cm. — (Thorndike Press large print western)
 ISBN-13: 978-1-4104-3549-1 (hardcover)
 ISBN-10: 1-4104-3549-0 (hardcover)
 1. Large type books. I. Title.
PS3573.E8224D43 2011
813'.54—dc22   2010048749

Published in 2011 by arrangement with NAL Signet, a member of Penguin Group (USA) Inc.

Printed in the United States of America
1 2 3 4 5 6 7 15 14 13 12 11

THE IMMORTAL COWBOY

This is respectfully dedicated to the "American Cowboy." His was the saga sparked by the turmoil that followed the Civil War, and the passing of more than a century has by no means diminished the flame.

True, the old days and the old ways are but treasured memories, and the old trails have grown dim with the ravages of time, but the spirit of the cowboy lives on.

In my travels — to Texas, Oklahoma, Kansas, Nebraska, Colorado, Wyoming, New Mexico, and Arizona — I always find something that reminds me of the Old West. While I am walking these plains and mountains for the first time, there is this feeling that a part of me is eternal, that I have known these old trails before. I believe it is the undying spirit of the frontier calling, allowing me, through the mind's eye, to step back into time. What is the appeal of the Old West of the American frontier?

It has been epitomized by some as the dark and bloody period in American history. Its heroes — Crockett, Bowie, Hickok, Earp — have been reviled and criticized. Yet the Old West lives on, larger than life.

It has become a symbol of freedom, when there was always another mountain to climb and another river to cross; when a dispute between two men was settled not with expensive lawyers, but with fists, knives, or guns. Barbaric? Maybe. But some things never change. When the cowboy rode into the pages of American history, he left behind a legacy that lives within the hearts of us all.

— *Ralph Compton*

CHAPTER 1

"Well, hell, I didn't need this."

Charlie Pike let his hand holding the letter drop to his side.

"Bad news, boss?"

"You could say that." He balled up the single sheet of paper and tossed it to his foreman. "Read it your own self, Billy."

Standing in dust, Bill Childes let go of the smoking branding iron he was holding and bent his head to the crumpled paper.

A hesitant forefinger slowly tracing the words, Childes read: " 'Major . . . come . . . quick. I need . . . you.' " He looked at Pike. "From Brig Gen Ret . . . d —"

"Brigadier General, Retired," Pike said.

"Gives his name as Henry J. Dryden. Then it says, 'Judge, Federal District Court, Breeze, northern New Mexico Territory.' "

Recognition dawned in Childes' eyes as he lifted them from the letter. "Wait a minute, I've heard tell of this man, boss.

7

You recollect the black wrangler you hired one time; name was Small or something like that? He had a simple son?"

"Yeah, I remember. It was a few years back."

"Well, Small, oncet he had three simple sons, until Judge Dryden hung two of them for breaking a peace officer's jaw and chicken stealing."

"Where the hell is Breeze, Billy?" Pike said.

"As I recollect, it's up on the San Juan River, close to the Old Spanish Trail," Childes said. "Last time I was in New Mexico, I left in a hurry, so I wasn't taking time to see the sights."

The foreman's critical eye watched a couple of drovers bring in a bunch of yearlings; then he turned back to Pike.

"From what I've heard, Dryden is a mean old snake and every time he rattles, a man ends up dangling. In the territory, they call him Hangin' Hank. He's strung up more'n his share, I can tell you."

Pike smiled. "Who told you this? The no-account outlaws I see loafing around the ranch all the time?"

"They're my friends, boss, an' they don't lie to me. Judge Dryden is a mean old buzzard and a hanging judge from way back.

He's got more enemies than the devil at a Baptist convention."

Childes waited for an answer, got none and said: "So?"

"So what?" Pike said.

"So you ain't going, are you?"

"I don't have any choice, Billy," Pike said. "During the war, the old man saved my life. I owe him."

"Boss, when a man like Hangin' Hank calls in a favor, he's in big trouble, an' you can bet your bottom dollar that means gun trouble," Childes said.

"Maybe not," Pike said. "It could be a legal problem."

"Right," Childes said. "A federal judge has a legal problem, so he calls in a Texas cowman for help. That's not the way of it, boss."

"Like I said, I owe him. I got it to do, Billy."

"Then for God's sake take Sanchez," Childes said. "He's the best around with the iron."

"I need Sanchez here for the roundup, Billy and you too," Pike said.

"Then you're going alone?"

"Yup. I reckon so."

"When?"

"Now," Pike said. "As soon as I saddle a

horse and pick up some grub from the cookhouse."

"What about Maxine?" Childes said.

"What about her?" Pike said.

"Will you tell her?"

"Of course," Pike said. "I'll swing past the schoolhouse before I leave." He smiled. "Take care of things while I'm gone, huh?"

"Boss, I've got a bad feeling about this," Childes said. "Right here, in the pit of my stomach."

"Kind of like a cold emptiness?" Pike said.

"Yeah, that's right. Empty, like, and icy cold, deep down in my gut."

"I know," Pike said. "I've got it too."

Maxine Holt stood outside the schoolhouse door. Inside, her dozen students had decided this was a perfect time to raise hell.

"You're wearing a gun, Charlie," she said, looking up at Pike in the saddle. "I've never seen you wear one before."

"I hear the Apaches are out, Maxine," Pike said. "A man can't be too careful." He smiled. "Though they're probably in the Madres by now."

"The war ended fifteen years ago, Charlie," Maxine said, returning to the subject they'd been discussing earlier. "It's too late for any man to be calling in favors."

"A man's obligation lasts a lifetime, Maxine," Pike said. "I can't turn my back on the general, not now."

"Then for God's sake send Pete Sanchez," Maxine said. "He's a gunfighter and he can take care of himself."

"It's not Pete's responsibility, it's mine."

"But you're expecting gunplay," Maxine said.

"Not really," Pike said. "But it's a long way from here to the San Juan. Besides, I may have to shoot my own chuck along the trail."

"Charlie," Maxine said, "you don't need a Colt's gun for that."

"I got to be going," Pike said. "I want to cover ground before dark."

The sky was blue, the sun high and to the west the Pecos River was a saber blade of glittering steel.

"I wasn't going to tell you right away until I was sure, but I'm late, Charlie," Maxine said. "Maybe two weeks."

Pike was silent; then he said: "Two weeks isn't long."

"It's not?" Maxine said. "So suddenly you're a woman and you know these things?"

"I don't know much about women. What do you want me to do, Maxine?"

11

"Stay here with me. I need you and we have to talk."

"I got to be going, Maxine. I won't be gone long. Less than a month, maybe so."

"A month!" Maxine said. "And in the meantime what happens to me? I want a ring and the kid needs a name."

"We'll get married when I get back," Pike said. "I promise."

He swung his horse away and behind him Maxine yelled: "Charlie Pike, you rotten, no-good, son of a bitch! Get back here!"

He didn't think Maxine was really that mad. But the rock that whizzed past his head convinced him otherwise.

CHAPTER 2

At noon, eleven days later, Charlie Pike cut the Old Spanish Trail a couple of miles northwest of Santa Fe.

He rode through the eroded Badland Hills standing more than seven thousand feet above the flat, spires and hoodoos of sandstone rock standing like silent sentinels, watching his progress.

The day was hot, but though he'd refilled his canteen in Santa Fe, Pike used his water sparingly. He had no idea if there was any more to be had until he reached the San Juan.

Around him stretched a vast, empty land where nothing moved and the only sounds were the footfalls of his sorrel and the creak of saddle leather. There was no breeze to curb the relentless sun and both he and the horse smelled rank of sweat.

Pike cleared the hills, rode into a wilderness of cactus and broken rock, cut through by thick arrowheads of piñon and juniper.

Behind him, ten miles to the east, the forested San Pedro Mountains looked cool as mint, their peaks framed against a julep-colored sky.

He was thinking about Maxine.

Two weeks late. That didn't sound like much. But he reminded himself she was talking about a monthly event and then suddenly it did.

When he got back, it would be six weeks, near enough and by then the fat would truly be in the fire.

He wouldn't be surprised if Maxine was pregnant.

She left her schoolma'am demeanor at the bedroom door. In the sack she was a biting, scratching, dirty-talking whore and anything went and for as long as Pike wanted it, an hour, a day, a week . . .

And Maxine was pretty, right pretty, all that yellow hair and cornflower blue eyes and a body that could keep a man awake at nights, remembering.

Did he love her? Away from bed did he even know her?

She never talked about her past, leaving it buried on a trail behind her. She'd just showed up in town one day, asked for the schoolteacher's job and got it. Then Pike had met her in the general store and that had been that.

He glanced at the sky, blue tinged with bands of pale red. But the sun was still high, scorching.

All right, he asked it again: Did he love her?

Pike began to build houses on a bridge he hadn't crossed yet. He enjoyed having sex with her, no doubt about that. But was it enough to hold on to, especially after a kid arrived?

And Maxine had a temper, flares of crimson-faced rage that usually ended up with her throwing at him whatever came to hand. Suppose one day she picked up a revolving gun and cut loose?

Or suppose she got fat or lost her teeth or her hair all fell out? What then?

Pike bowed his head, ashamed of his traitorous thoughts.

And saved his life.

The bullet blew his hat six feet into the air. He dived off the horse, hit the ground hard and rolled behind a rock.

A cackle from somewhere ahead of him, then: "Did I git you, sonny?"

"You sorry piece of shit!" Pike yelled. "Why did you try to kill me?"

"I want your sorrel, boy. My own pony is well nigh wore out, on account he warn't much to begin with."

Another shot caromed viciously off the top of the rock.

The man's voice again. "Step into the open and take your medicine, sonny. I don't have all day, now."

"You go to hell," Pike said.

"Well, I'll kill you if'n you do step out, an' I'll kill you if'n you don't. It's all the same to me," the man said. "Stepping out is quicker, is all."

Maxine forgotten, Pike drew his Colt and looked around him.

To his left was wide-open ground, broken up by a few yuccas. To his right lay fifty yards of level sand, then a slanted stratum of yellow and tan rock that rose to a height of about twenty feet above the flat. It then stretched away into the distance, gradually gaining elevation.

If there was a way to outflank the bushwhacker, that was the route to take. That is, if he could cover fifty yards of open ground and climb into the rocks without getting dropped in his tracks.

Pike played for time.

"You with the rifle, let's talk about this," he said.

16

"Nothing to talk about, sonny," the man said. "You got a hoss and I'm willing to kill you to get it."

The sorrel was grazing on bunchgrass about twenty yards away, seemingly unconcerned by the gunfire.

"All right, I'm done," Pike said. "I'm all shot to pieces here. Come and get the horse."

"I ain't that green, boy," the man said. He cackled again.

Pike grimaced. Where the heck was the voice coming from?

"Hey you, we got a standoff here," Pike said. "You can't get me and I can't get you."

"Maybe so," the man said. "But come dark I'll get you all right. See, I'm half Apache, half wildcat an' all son of a bitch an' I can see like a cat in the dark."

"Yeah, you're a son of a bitch all right," Pike said.

The bushwhacker cackled.

Minutes passed, stretched into an hour. The shadows lengthened but the sun was still hot and Pike was tormented by thirst. His canteen was hanging from the horn of the sorrel's saddle.

He tried to whistle the horse closer. It raised its head, looked at him briefly, then went back to grazing.

17

"No escape thataway, sonny," the bush-whacker said.

"Damn you, I'm thirsty," Pike said.

"You won't be for much longer," the man said.

Pike wiped his right hand on his jeans, then palmed the Colt again.

"Throw me down a canteen," he said.

Pike got ready, his legs under him.

A giggle, then: "I already done tol' you, boy, I ain't that green."

"Who the hell are you?" Pike said. His voice was dry and croaky.

"Name's Ephraim Satin, originally out of Bent's Fort up Coloraddy way, but now I get around."

Pike clutched at a straw. "I'm close kin to Judge Henry J. Dryden of this territory," he said. "Satin, he'll hang you fer sure."

The man laughed. "Ol' Hangin' Hank ain't stringin' up anybody, boy. No more, he ain't. He's lying abed with a cancer gnawin' on his belly. I heard that."

"You heard wrong," Pike said.

"Well, anyways, he ain't here," the man said. "Is he, now?"

The day was slowly shading into evening, the shadows were growing and the blue denim sky was streaked with ribbons of scarlet and jade. A breeze ruffled the trees, carrying with it the tang of sage and the dusty scent of hot rock.

Pike studied the stratum of rock to his right. As soon as it got dark, he'd make his move.

A bullet chipped the top of Pike's sheltering boulder; then two more kicked up exclamation points of sand on either side of him.

"Jes' keepin' you honest, boy," the bushwhacker said. "Like maybe you was plannin' on makin' a run fer the rocks or some sich tomfoolery."

Pike spat dust. Whatever other talents Ephraim Satin possessed, one of them was obviously mind reader.

Then he'd wait for Satin to come to him. An Apache, especially a half-Apache, could die like any other man.

Now Pike wished he'd brought Pete Sanchez with him. He was slick with the iron and he could hit a man far off. But Pete was back in Texas, rounding up cows.

"Hey, sonny," the bushwhacker said.

"The name's Charlie," Pike said.

"You got a good head of hair, Charlie?" the man said.

"I got enough."

"Good," the man said, "I aim to take that as well."

19

Angry, Pike rose, thumbed a probing shot into the shadowed land in front of him. An answering bullet hit the rock to his right, driving ragged chips into his side. He quickly dived down again, bleeding.

He wouldn't try that a second time.

CHAPTER 3

"Hey, Charlie," the man called Satin said.

"What do you want?"

"It's gettin' dark," Satin said. "If you got any prayers, now's the time to start sayin' them."

"I got me a Colt's gun," Pike said. "And Texans don't die that easy."

"Charlie, a Colt's gun ain't gonna make the difference," Satin said. "I can cut a man's throat so fast, when he gets to hell, he ain't even started bleedin' yet."

"You're a talking man, Satin," Pike said. "It's going to be the death of you one day."

A cackle. "One day, maybe, but not today, Charlie, not today."

The sky had shaded to lilac and sentinel stars stood watch. Among the rocks a pair of hunting coyotes called back and forth and the rising breeze whispered its false promises to the trees.

"Charlie!"

"Yeah?"

"I got to be going," Satin said. "It's time for me to make camp, bile coffee, an' fry up a mess o' bacon. On account of all that, I'll kill you real soon."

"Or I'll kill you," Pike said.

"I got no fear o' that, Charlie," Satin said. "You're a rube, boy. I seen that right off."

Pike raised his Colt and listened into the night. He heard only the wind and the yipping coyotes.

Then he recalled what General Dryden had told him one time. "Major Pike, when you find yourself in a tight situation, do what the enemy least expects, then fight him on a ground of your own choosing."

Satin would expect him to stay where he was or try to lose himself in the rocks and piñon. He would do neither.

It was dark enough.

Crouching low, he stepped on cat feet toward what he guessed had been the hidden gunman's position. Tired of cowering behind a rock like a frightened rabbit, he planned on taking the fight directly to Satin.

The moon was up, blading bone white among the rocks and trees. Around Pike the shadows were dark, menacing, filled with uneasy movement.

Ahead of him, a shower of debris rolled

across stone. Pike froze, brought up his Colt, his heart hammering.

"Sceer ya, Charlie, boy?"

Satin's voice, off to his right somewhere in the darkness. Pike made no sound. The man wanted him to give his position away.

Pike touched his tongue to his dry top lip. He must bring him out. Lure Satin into the open.

He backed away, head turning, searching the crowding gloom for his horse. Pike stepped slowly, carefully, aware that a snapping twig or a loose rock could draw a bullet.

The coyotes were hunting closer and a stray cloud covered the face of the moon. A night bird called, called again, then fell silent.

Pike was walking with death, making his fearful way through the opalescent night. Again he was wishful for Sanchez, for his rifle, for water, for a way out.

But he had none of those things.

The big sorrel was grazing among clumps of prickly pear, its reins trailing. The moon was again clear, as round as a coin, spreading its blanched light.

A horse is a notional animal. Sometimes it will shy away from the approach of a rider, other times trot toward him with every show of welcome. To Pike's relief, the sorrel did the latter.

He gathered up the reins, swung into the saddle and slid the Winchester from the boot. Expecting a bullet at any second, he took a few moments to ponder his options.

He could skedaddle. But the ground behind him was broken and rocky and it would slow him to a walk, an easy target for Satin's rifle.

Ahead of him was a stretch of open ground, long enough to run the horse, turn and run again. The sound of hooves would bring Satin out.

Or so he hoped.

Pike glanced at the grinning moon, then levered a round into the rifle, immediately drawing fire. A bullet split the air close to his head and another slammed into his saddle horn.

The time for pondering was over.

Yodeling a Rebel yell, Pike kicked the sorrel into motion. The big horse lurched forward and broke into a gallop. Ahead of him, he saw Satin, a gray, whiskery man in buckskins, step from behind the boulder that had sheltered him earlier.

Pike threw the rifle to his shoulder and fired. The Winchester's iron sights were invisible in the darkness and he could only point and shoot. His bullet missed, but clipped close enough to drive Satin to one knee.

Pike worked his rifle and now he was opposite the man. Then Satin surprised the hell out of him.

A tomahawk spun through the air and missed braining Pike by inches. But the beard of the blade sliced along the side of his jaw, nicked the lobe of his right ear and furrowed across his scalp.

Stunned, he tumbled backward out of the saddle, his rifle cartwheeling away from him. He landed hard on his back. And lay there, winded.

The shuffle of boots drew close to Pike. Then Satin's voice, faintly mocking. "I aim to kill you now, Charlie."

Those seven short words gave Pike all the time he needed.

His Colt was still in the holster and he drew and fired, just as Satin raised his rifle. Pike's bullet hit the side plate of the Winchester and ranged upward, hitting Satin high in his skinny chest.

Pike fired again, aiming for the man's belly, and Satin staggered and went down.

Rising to his feet, his cheek and throat sticky with blood, Pike walked toward Satin, kicked his rifle away, then relieved the man of his belt gun and knife.

Satin looked up at him. He looked old, a wrinkled graybeard with faded eyes.

"Ye got me, Charlie," he said. "I never thought you had it in you, boy."

Pike smiled. "Old man, I fit Yankees that were a sight meaner than you."

"You're fast with the iron, Charlie," Satin said.

"Not where I come from," Pike said.

"Then I talk too much. Gave you time."

"I told you it would be the death of you one day."

"I need my pipe," Satin said. "Drag me to the rock over yonder."

Pike propped the man against the boulder and watched while Satin lit his pipe. "Bile me coffee, Charlie," he said. "I don't reckon they have Arbuckles' in hell."

"Old man, I don't owe you a thing," Pike said.

"You done kilt me," Satin said. "Ain't that worth a thing?"

"No, damn you, it's nothing." He shook his head. "All right, I'll bile up some coffee."

Pike walked to the rock stratum. It was much steeper than he'd imagined and if he'd tried to climb it he'd now be a dead man.

26

But to his joy, a thin trickle of water ran from a crevice in the sandstone. It took him a few minutes to fill the coffeepot and by that time Satin was dead.

Pike brought in his horse and camped by the water. At first light he searched among the rocks where Satin had holed up, found his canteen and horse, a small, swaybacked mustang and dabbed a rope on him.

Two days later, leading the mustang, he rode into the town of Breeze.

CHAPTER 4

The settlement sprawled along the south bank of the San Juan, its single street flanked by timber and adobe buildings of no great size.

But Breeze had some pretensions to gentility.

It had a brick courthouse, a school and a white-painted church. The permanent gallows standing next to the courthouse detracted from the tranquil scene, but it lacked paint and the usual red, white and blue bunting and looked as though it had not been used in some time.

Pike had a six-beer thirst, but taking care of his horse first was the habit of a lifetime. The livery stood on the edge of town, the usual location ordained by city fathers who wanted to cut down on the number of summer flies.

The hour was still early and the only people on the street were merchants opening their stores, a few matronly women and a drunk headed into a saloon.

But as he passed a false-fronted mercantile, a man's voice hailed him from the boardwalk. "Hold up there, mister."

A tall man with a sweeping dragoon mustache and a hard eye regarded him without pleasure. He wore a five-pointed star on his leather vest and a holstered Colt on his hip.

"What can I do for you, Sheriff?" Pike said.

"It's marshal. Nathan McLeod is the name."

"Then, what can I do for you, Marshal?"

"You're leading Ephraim Satin's hoss," McLeod said.

"Seems like."

"Where's Satin?"

"Dead."

"You kill him?" McLeod said.

"Yeah, a couple of days ago," Pike said.

"Satin was an old mountain man. You can kill a mountain man in a straight-up fight, but he'll get a bullet into you."

Pike turned and showed his bloody cheek. "He tried it with a tomahawk."

"Why did you kill him?" McLeod said.

"He wanted to trade his pony for mine," Pike said.

"You were getting the worst of that bargain."

"I know, but Satin didn't see it that way."

"He's got friends in this town," McLeod said.

Pike nodded. "And I'm sure they're all fine, upstanding citizens just like he was."

McLeod let that go and said: "You passing through?" He smiled thinly. "Let me rephrase that: You are passing through."

Pike waited until a brewery wagon rumbled past, then said: "Judge Dryden sent for me."

"So you're the one," McLeod said. He looked over Pike's tall, lanky frame and worn, dusty range clothes. "You're not what I expected."

"What did you expect, Marshal?" Pike said.

"Oh, I don't know. A gunfighter, maybe."

"I'm not a gunfighter. I'm a rancher."

"Yeah, shows on you," McLeod said. He pointed up the street. "The judge's house is just beyond the courthouse. He lives with a whore who goes by the name of Loretta Lamont. I got a deputy posted outside, one of two I hired at sixty a month to protect the old man. The mayor is thrilled about that."

"Protect him?" Pike said. "Protect him

from what?"

"There's been seven attempts on Dryden's life in the past six-month, mostly by kinfolk of the hundred men he's hung over the years. I've killed three men in that six-month and crippled another, all of them young, lively lads. I don't want to have to kill another."

McLeod stared at Pike. "The judge cleaned up this part of the territory all right, but he didn't know when the time had come to stop the hanging."

Pike's voice was forced. "Is that what he wants me to do? Protect him?"

"I don't know," McLeod said. "But whatever he wants, don't let the sun go down on your ass tonight with it still in Breeze. You comprehend me, mister?"

"I'll talk to him," Pike said.

"Yeah, you do that," McLeod said. "But remember what I told you. If you're still in town after dark, I'll gun you. I got enough troublemakers here as it is."

Pike rubbed a hand over his stubbled chin. The beer could wait. He'd talk to the general first.

He touched his hat. "Much obliged for the friendly welcome, Marshal."

"Cowboy, Dryden should have stopped the hanging before he strung up Clem

Dredge's brother," McLeod said. "Clem took that hard and he's one of them aiming to kill him. The only difference is, when Clem says he'll do a thing, he gets it done. And he'll gun anybody stands in his way."

"Then why don't you arrest him, Marshal?" Pike said.

"Clem Dredge is an outlaw and the fastest gun in the New Mexico Territory," McLeod said. "I'll give you my badge and you go arrest him."

"Not my job," Pike said. He kneed his horse into motion.

"Remember what I told you," McLeod said to Pike's retreating back. "You got until sundown."

CHAPTER 5

Judge Henry J. Dryden lived in a modest, clapboard house set on a fenced lot that grew nothing but dust and cactus. There was a barn out back.

A sour deputy with a beard down to the buckle of his gun belt stood at the gate. He measured Pike with his eyes, then picked up the Greener shotgun that was leaning against the fence.

"Stay right where you're at, mister," he said. "I got faith in this here scattergun."

Pike drew rein. "I'm here to see Judge Dryden."

"A lot o' folks want to see Judge Dryden," the man said.

"Name's Charlie Pike. The judge and me served in the army together."

"You wore the gray?" the man said.

Pike nodded. "General Dryden was my commanding officer."

"Wore the gray my own self," the man

said. He turned his head. "Loretta!"

No answer. He tried again. "Loretta!"

The door swung open. A young, blond woman stood framed in the doorway. "What the heck is all the yelling about, Deke?"

"Feller here goes by the name of Charlie Pike. Says he wants to see the judge."

"He's expected," Loretta said. "Let him pass."

"Climb down slow, mister," Deke said. "I'm not what you'd call a trusting man."

Pike swung out of the saddle and tethered the horses to the hitching rail.

"While you're at it, hang your gun belt there as well," Deke said.

Pike smiled. "You're surely not a trusting man, are you?"

"Live longer that way," Deke said. He watched Pike stash his gun belt, then motioned with the shotgun. "Step inside."

The woman at the door gave Pike the once-over, seemed less than unimpressed, then said: "My name is Miss Loretta Lamont. I'm Judge Dryden's companion."

"How is he?" Pike said.

"Low, but hanging on."

"Why did he send for me?" Pike said.

"Ask him," Loretta said. She turned. "Follow me."

Lying between white sheets, Dryden

looked like a scrawny scarecrow that had fallen in snow.

He raised a blue-veined hand. "I knew you'd come, Major Pike."

"I owe you, General."

The judge smiled. "Ah yes, the Wilderness. That was a fight."

"One I'd rather forget," Pike said.

"Loretta, my dear," Dryden said, "you never saw a man more covered in maggots than Major Pike was the day I found him."

"Eeoow," Loretta said, making a face.

"They helped save him, though," Dryden said. "Ate up all the gangrene."

Anticipating another screech from Loretta, Pike said quickly: "Why did you send for me, General?"

Dryden waved. "Take a seat, Major, by the wall there. Can I get you a drink?"

"The war is long over. Please call me Charlie," Pike said.

"Very well, Charlie. And you may call me Judge. Now, about that drink?"

"I could use a cold beer," Pike said, taking his seat.

"Loretta, do we have any cold beer?" Dryden said.

"Only warm beer," Loretta said.

"That will do fine," Pike said.

Dryden watched Loretta's hips sway from

the bedroom, then said: "Fine girl, Loretta. Takes good care of me." He looked at Pike. "I'm dying, Charlie."

"I'm sorry to find you so low, Judge," Pike said.

"Age and disease come to all of us. I already see gray hair at your temples."

Dryden let the silence stretch, then said: "I don't want to be buried here, in foreign soil. I want you to take me back to Texas so that my bones may rest in peace."

"Judge, the marshal —"

"Nathan McLeod."

"Yeah, him. He wants me out of town by nightfall."

"And so you shall be," Dryden said. "We'll leave within the hour." He watched the woman reenter the room. "And Loretta will come, of course."

Pike took the bottle Loretta handed to him. "Judge, are you well enough to ride?"

"With Texas on my horizon, I can ride," Dryden said.

The beer was warm, but wet. Pike drank and said: "Why Charlie Pike?"

"Because I need a man I can trust," Dryden said. "You were a fine officer and I can trust you."

"McLeod told me about Clem Dredge," Pike said. "It seems Dredge wants your scalp, Judge."

"Our esteemed city marshal is a killer," Dryden said. "And he loves to talk about other killers."

Loretta laughed, the false, cracked bell of the saloon girl. "Nate McLeod only told you half of it. Did he tell you who's riding with Dredge?"

Pike shook his head.

"John Martin Simpson," Loretta said.

"You mean J. M. Simpson, out of Kansas?"

"That would be the man," Loretta said, a gleam in her eyes.

Pike sat back in his chair and took a long pull of beer. "They say he's killed a dozen men," he said.

"They say right," Loretta said.

"A very dangerous man indeed," Dryden said. "Does this mean you'll turn tail, Charlie?"

"I'll stick," Pike said, instantly regretting the words. "I'll take you as far as the Texas border."

"No, Charlie, you'll take me to Waco on the Brazos," Dryden said. "I have friends there and the town is close to your ranch."

A man who'd just run out of room on the dance floor, Pike nodded.

"Excellent," Dryden said. "Loretta will

serve you another beer in the parlor while I ready myself for the journey."

Pike followed Loretta into the parlor, over-ornately furnished in the accepted fashion of the time.

The woman brought him another beer and said: "What are our chances of getting the judge to the Brazos alive?"

"I don't know," Pike said. "But I sense hard times coming down."

"Then why do it?" Loretta said.

"I owe him."

"Cowboy," Loretta said, "sometimes the price of repaying a debt comes too high."

CHAPTER 6

"Lock the door, Loretta, my dear," Dryden said. "Remember, this house will be yours soon."

Looking like death, Dryden sat a buckskin horse and watched Loretta lock the door and put the brass key in her purse.

"Good, then we're ready to leave," Dryden said. "Loretta, my strongbox is in my saddle-bags?"

"Just like you ordered, Henry."

"Good, then we're all set to go."

Dryden did not wear a belt gun but had a .44 Henry rifle booted under his left knee.

Pike doubted that the man could heft the Henry's nine-pound weight.

Loretta hitched up her skirts and climbed onto the back of a paint mustang. Once settled, she opened a white parasol over her head.

The sun was high in the sky, the heat intense and the air smelled of dust. "Nothing like letting the whole town know we're leaving," Pike said.

"Day or night, Dredge would know anyway," Loretta said. "He's got friends in town."

The deputy stepped beside Dryden's horse. "Good luck, Judge," he said. "I didn't like this damned job anyhow."

"Why, thank you, Deke," Dryden said. "How is the little lady?"

"Better now spring is here," Deke said. "The rheumatisms punish her in cold weather."

"Glad to hear she's feeling better," Dryden said. "Give her my regards."

"I sure will, Judge," Deke said.

Marshal Nathan McLeod was standing on the boardwalk. "You're leaving, Judge?" he said.

"Yes, Nate," Dryden said. "Headed for Texas. I will not be laid to rest in this ground."

"Man does what he thinks is right," McLeod said.

"Where is Dredge, Marshal?" Pike asked.

McLeod waved a hand. "Out there, someplace."

Pike nodded. "We'll be taking the Old Spanish Trail. It's the fastest route."

"Good as any," McLeod said. "Steer clear

of Apaches."

"I aim to," Pike said. "I left Satin's horse at the judge's house, if anyone wants to claim it."

"The glue factory, probably," McLeod said. "I'll take care of it."

"Well, farewell, then, Marshal McLeod," Dryden said. "And thank you for your years of loyal service to my court."

"My pleasure, Judge," McLeod said. He touched his hat brim and grinned. "Miss Loretta."

They had almost cleared the edge of town before Pike looked back. McLeod stood in the street, watching them.

"The last place on earth we'll head for is the Spanish Trail," Pike said. "And I think McLeod knows it."

"If he knows, Clem Dredge will know," Loretta said.

"Which might be all to the good," Dryden said.

Pike wondered at that.

Riding through the shimmering heat of the day, Pike headed due south, into flat tablelands that rose seven hundred feet above the flat.

Piñon, juniper, mountain mahogany and manzanita grew everywhere and sagebrush and prickly pear choked the arroyos.

Here the air was thinner and harder to breathe, heavily scented with sage and pine.

After another five miles they rode up on a deep canyon. Pike dismounted and stepped to the rim.

"Can we pass?" Dryden said.

Pike made no answer.

"Charlie," Dryden said again, "can we pass?"

"I see a switchback game trail that heads to the bottom," Pike said.

"Can we use it?" Dryden said.

Pike looked around him, at a wilderness of rock and trees. On both sides of him the canyon stretched away forever. On his left its steep walls angled to the southeast, then were lost in haze.

"We can't go around it," Pike said.

"Oh, for heaven's sake, Charlie," Loretta said, her face flushed under her parasol. "Can we get across? Tell us yes or no."

"We can take the game trail," Pike said. Then, after a moment of silence: "If we dismount and lead the horses."

He looked at Dryden. "Are you up for that, Judge?"

"I'll manage."

"It's steep."

"I told you, I'll manage." More sharply.

"One more thing," Pike said. "There's smoke to the southeast."

"Apaches?" Loretta sounded alarmed.

"I doubt it."

"Why?" Loretta said.

"Way too much smoke," Pike said.

"Charlie," Dryden said, "I have a ship's glass in my saddlebags. Take a closer look."

Pike found the large, brass telescope and scanned the far side of the canyon.

"What do you see?" Loretta said.

Without removing the glass from his eye, Pike said: "It's a settlement of some kind. Four, no, five adobes at the base of a bluff."

He palmed the telescope shut. "Maybe we can add to our supplies."

"We have to get over there first," Loretta said.

Pike nodded. "Yeah, there's that."

"Then let's quit jawing and get it done," Dryden said. "We've got ground to cover between here and Texas."

The way down was not as difficult as Pike had feared. The switchback was fairly wide and gave his horse no difficulty. Behind him Dryden and Loretta made little complaint.

As they dropped lower, the air became humid and the bottom of the canyon was shadowed and marshy, supporting willows, cottonwoods, cattails and juniper. Wild grapevines laced the walls and fields of tomatillos grew everywhere in swaths of bright green.

Pike thought the canyon a pleasant place, a shady spot where a man could linger and enjoy its quiet solitude. But Dryden's voice, rustling like dry parchment, dispelled the mood.

"Find us a way out of this hellhole, Charlie," he said.

Loretta had picked a pink wildflower and she'd stuck it in her hair.

"Very becoming, Loretta," Pike said, smiling.

"Shut up, Charlie," Loretta said. "Get me out of this damned canyon."

Pike's smile slipped. It seemed nothing about this trip boded well.

And this was only the beginning.

CHAPTER 7

The climb to the canyon's south rim was not demanding. But there were no game trails and it took longer, mainly because Pike was forced to turn back and try another route when rocks or a crevasse barred their way.

When they were on the flat again, Loretta mounted her paint, then brushed a strand of hair from her forehead. "I need a drink," she said.

Dryden smiled. "My dear, perhaps the settlement ahead has a cantina."

"I sure as hell hope so, Henry," she said.

Dryden looked at Pike. "Lead on, Charlie."

The closer they drew to the settlement, the less Pike liked what he saw.

The place was dirty, slovenly and run-down. Pigs wallowed in mud in front of the jacales, a couple of naked children among them and, close by, the rusted iron blades of a water windmill screeched like the newly damned.

A man wearing a filthy vest stood at the door of a jacal and watched Pike and the others come. He shaded his eyes with a hand for a few moments, then quickly ducked inside.

Pike turned in the saddle. "Judge, I don't like this. Something doesn't set right with me."

"What do you suggest, Charlie?" Dryden said.

"We turn around and keep on riding," Pike said.

"The place seems all right to me," Loretta said. "I bet they got mescal."

"The lady wants a drink, Charlie," Dryden said.

"Not here," Pike said.

"Damn it, Charlie," Loretta said, "there's nothing else between this dump and the Brazos."

Pike drew rein. "Not here. I got a bad feeling coming down on me."

"Then you stay here," Loretta said. "Me and the judge will ride in by ourselves."

Pike looked at Dryden. "Judge?"

The old man shrugged. "I could use some coffee."

"Well," Loretta said, "what are we waiting for?"

"Wait," Pike said. He drew his Colt and thumbed a shell into the empty chamber that had been under the hammer.

"You are worried, Charlie." Dryden smiled.

"More than worried, Judge," Pike said. "A mite scared."

"Lookee there," Loretta said. "I told you this dump would have a cantina."

A hand-lettered sign over the door of the largest adobe said:

CANTINA
Jas. Lee Prop.

"Jas Lee Prop," Loretta said. "You figure he's a Chinaman?"

"My dear," Dryden said, "the sign means that the proprietor of this fine establishment is a gentleman by the name of James Lee."

"Oh, is that all?" Loretta said.

Pike sat his horse and looked around him.

A slatternly woman with stringy blond hair came to the door of a jacal, watching them, a small child clinging to her skirts. She shooed the kid inside, rounded up another and did the same with him. The door slammed shut and Pike heard a bolt slam.

"Friendly folks," he said.

But Dryden and Loretta had already dismounted and did not hear him. Reluctantly he swung out of the saddle. There was no hitching rail and he let the sorrel's reins trail.

Inside, the cantina was dark and hot and smelled of piss, sweat and cheap whiskey.

Pike heard grunting from the other end of the room and at first thought a pig was inside. But as his eyes grew accustomed to the gloom, he made out the shape of a man humping on top of a woman who was sprawled on her back. Another man sat close by, watching without noticeable interest.

"And what can I do for you nice people?"

The man in the filthy vest whom Pike had seen at the door stood behind a bar that consisted of a timber plank thrown across a couple of sawhorses.

"Are you Jas Lee Prop?" Loretta asked.

"Indeed I am, young lady. And what can I do for you?"

"Any mescal?"

"Nope."

"Tequila?"

"Nope."

"Brandy?"

"Nope."

"Then what the heck do you have?"

"Whiskey, in the barrel there," Lee said. "Eighteen gallons of genuine Carrizo Canyon busthead."

"Let's have at it, then," Loretta said. She looked at Dryden. "Judge?"

The sun blindness had cleared from Pike's eyes. Over at the far end of the saloon, the screwing man had slowed down, taking his time. The woman's face was turned to Pike. She looked bored.

"Is that really necessary?" Dryden asked the bartender, nodding toward the couple.

Lee shrugged. "Too hot outside. Gotta do it somewhere." He poured a drink for Loretta, then said to Dryden: "What kind of judge are you?"

"A none-of-your-damned-business kind of judge," Pike said. He motioned to Loretta. "Drink up. We're leaving."

"Stow it, Charlie," Loretta said. "We'll tell you when we're leaving."

Dryden smiled. "Bartender, I'll have coffee."

"Comin' up." He looked at Pike. "You?"

"Nothing."

"Hard to please, huh?"

"Not much to please a man in this place,"

Pike said.

"I could take that as an insult," Lee said. His eyes were ugly.

"Take it any way you want," Pike said.

Anger spiked in him.

He crossed the floor in three long strides and kicked the humping man hard in the ribs. "You, get off of her. I've seen enough."

The man rolled on his back, shocked. The woman pulled down her skirts and got to her feet.

Pike looked down at the man, a huge, shaggy bear with a red beard spreading across his chest. He smelled like a skunk.

Pike pointed to the man's crotch. "Put that little thing away," he said.

The man cursed, rose and buttoned his pants over his glistening member. "I'll kill you for that," he said.

His holstered gun was over the back of a chair and he dived for it. Suddenly Dryden was standing between them.

"My name is Judge Henry J. Dryden," he said. "If there's any killing done here, I'll see that the man responsible hangs for it."

Pike saw a significant glance exchange between the Bear and the man who'd been watching his performance.

He shook his head. That ripped it real

good. Dryden had just put their feet to the fire.

"Well, well, well, if it ain't ol' Hangin' Hank in the flesh as ever was," the Bear said. He buckled on his gun belt, then swept off his hat. "Pleased to make your acquaintance, Judge. I'm Jesse Thorne an' this here's my brother Elliot. The woman, well, I don't recollect her name."

Thorne waved a hand at the woman. "Get the hell out of here." He winked at the judge. "Gettin' mighty bored with the bitch. Takin' me all day to finish my business, know what I mean?"

His eyes moved beyond Dryden and he said, loud enough for Loretta to hear: "Now, that little lady over there would be a different story."

"Go screw yourself," Loretta said.

"Not when you're around." Thorne grinned.

"Got your coffee, Judge," Lee said from the bar.

Dryden nodded. "Mr. Thorne, have a drink on me and mind your affairs."

Thorne glared at his woman. "I thought I told you to get the hell out of here."

"You're still taking me with you, ain't you, Jesse?" the woman said.

"Maybe I'll keep you until I find some-

51

thing better," Jesse said. "And that might be real soon. Now beat it."

The woman gave Loretta a poisonous glance as she stepped out the door.

After it closed behind her, Thorne said: "I am minding my affairs, Judge. See, I mean to kill you very soon."

His eyes moved to Pike. "You're out of it, cowboy. You can ride on."

Elliot Thorne was on now his feet, as big, dirty and unkempt as his brother. He wore a Remington in a cross-draw holster. The rig looked handy.

Dryden smiled. He walked across to the bar and picked up his coffee with a bony, white hand that was as steady as a rock.

Without turning, he said: "Why would you want to kill me, Mr. Thorne? Did I hang one of your loved ones?"

Jesse grinned and spat. "Nah, I don't have any loved ones."

"Then why?" Dryden said.

"Because you're worth five hundred dollars to me," Jesse said. "Dead or alive."

"Ah," Dryden said. "And pray, who places such a low premium on my life?"

Jesse grinned again. "Hell, Judge, ol' Clem Dredge put out the word months ago. But providence," he said, joining his hands and rolling his eyes heavenward, "has placed you in my path."

"What about you, cowboy?" Elliot said. "You in or out?"

"Name's Pike and I'm in. I don't turn my back on no-good vermin like you."

"Your funeral," Elliot said. "And thanks to your big trap, you get it in the belly. Later we'll sit with a drink and watch you die."

"Charlie, you were right," Loretta said in a small voice. "Let's get out of here."

"Little lady, you're not going anywhere," Jesse said, smiling. "I got big plans for you and the floor behind me is part of them."

"Wait," Dryden said. "This can be settled. I always say that money talks all languages."

"That it does, Judge," Jesse said. "What do you have in mind?"

Dryden drained his cup. Suddenly he looked old and frail and sick.

"On my person I have five thousand dollars in cash," Dryden said. "It's yours, Mr. Thorne, if you will give us the road."

"Let's see your money," Jesse said.

"Judge," Pike said, "with trash like this, you can't buy your way out of trouble. They'll take your money and kill us anyway."

"No, Charlie," Dryden said. "I understand now that this is the only way."

He stepped closer to Jesse and put his

53

hand inside his frock coat. "The money is in my wallet," he said. "All of it."

Jesse grinned. "Let me have it, Judge."

"Certainly," Dryden said.

CHAPTER 8

Judge Dryden held out a large black wallet in his right hand.

Jesse Thorne yelled: "Yeehah!" and grabbed for the wallet. But Dryden let it drop.

In the last split second of his life, Jesse saw the twin muzzles of a Remington derringer pointed right between his eyes. His jaw dropped.

Dryden pulled the trigger and the bullet crashed square into Jesse's belly.

Elliot drew. Too slow. Dryden fired again and a red rose opened up on Elliot's forehead.

Both men were down, Elliot dead, Jesse screaming like a gutted hog.

Pike saw Jas Lee Prop bring up a scattergun from somewhere behind the bar. He fired, hit Lee in the chest and fired again. The man rammed backward into the whiskey barrel and tipped it over onto the floor.

The staves burst apart and Lee lay bleeding in a puddle of rotgut.

Dryden bent, picked up his wallet and put it back into his coat. He broke open the derringer, thumbed out the empty shells, then reloaded from his frock coat pocket.

He looked at Pike. "You are so correct, Charlie," he said. "One can't buy one's way out of gun trouble."

Loretta was at Dryden's side. "Are you all right, Henry?"

"Unscathed, my dear, as you can see," Dryden said.

She looked at Jesse. "He's not dead," she said.

"Not yet," Dryden said. "But he'll ride my bullet into hell soon enough."

He put a hand on Pike's shoulder. "Thank you, Charlie," he said. "You're fast with the iron."

"Not where I come from," Pike said. He felt slightly sick.

Loretta shuddered. "Let's get out of this dump."

"My dear, it will be dark soon," Dryden said. "We'll drag the carrion outside and spend the night here."

"Here?" Loretta said. "In this awful place?"

Dryden smiled. "I think a dirt floor will

be easier on my poor bones than sleeping on limestone rock."

He looked at Pike, then at the dead. "Will you do the honors?"

"I think we should move on," Pike said.

"I've shot and hanged a lot of men," Dryden said. "Not one of them has come back to haunt me."

"Clem Dredge will soon know we're here," Pike said. "If he doesn't know already."

"He's right, Henry," Loretta said. "I don't want to sleep here tonight."

Dryden gave a little bow. "Then I submit to the majority. We'll leave."

"Now, Henry, please," Loretta said.

As the judge and Loretta stepped outside, Pike looked at the bodies of the Thorne brothers. By any standard, Dryden's shooting had been excellent.

A derringer was a belly gun and mighty uncertain, but the judge had handled the piece like an expert.

Pike's thoughts went back to the war.

Dryden had risen through the ranks and had been regarded as a first-rate fighting man who led his troops from the front. He disdained the officer's sword and always carried a brace of Colts. And he'd killed his share.

He was a man to be reckoned with, then and now, Pike decided. And neither age nor sickness had made him any less dangerous.

Pike looked at Dryden standing outside the cantina door.

"Hell, Judge," he whispered to himself, "the way you shoot, you could have made this trip by your own self."

The question, niggling as a bedtime toothache, nagged at him.

Why hadn't he?

Dryden and Loretta were already mounted when Pike walked outside. He swung into the saddle and watched as Jesse's woman ran into the cantina.

An agonized screech followed from inside.

"It seems that even coyotes have someone to grieve for them," Dryden said, smiling.

At that moment, his face harsh, intolerant, unfeeling, he was Hangin' Hank, pronouncing his judgment.

Pike led the way south, riding through broken, hilly country that in places rose to eight thousand feet above the flat. Vast woodlands of piñon and juniper stretched away in all directions, nudging aside stands of sage, chaparral and yucca.

To the east, above the high mesa country,

blades of steel blue heat lightning branded a dark sky and the air had grown noticeably cooler.

The light of day was fading and shadows pooled among the hills.

"Canyon up ahead," Pike said.

"I know that canyon," Dryden said. "Or at least I've heard of it."

Pike turned in the saddle, his eyes asking a question.

"Largo Canyon," Dryden said. "I was told the Navajo made a stand there against the Spanish. It was way back when."

"We'll find a place to camp," Pike said. His gaze probed the distance ahead of him. "Tackle the canyon in the morning."

"Good," Loretta said. "I feel like I was born on the back of this pony."

"Derriere hurt, my dear?" Dryden asked.

"If you mean my ass, the answer is yeah. And I need a piss."

Dryden smiled his cadaver smile. "Loretta, you're such a charming little whore."

"I know, Henry," Loretta said. "That's why I wreck your damned bed every night and never hear you complain."

"Touché, my dear," Dryden said.

"There's a break in the trees over there," Pike said, nodding. "It could be a likely place."

"Lead on, Charlie," Loretta said. She kneed her horse in front of Dryden. "Whores first."

The clearing was a flat, grassy area between the piñon and a narrow stream ran close by, trickling over a sand and pebble bottom. A single cottonwood raised its smoky head above the piñon.

Loretta swung out of the saddle and fled for the trees, hitching her skirts as she ran.

"Think it might rain, Charlie?" Dryden asked.

"It might," Pike said. "Sometimes the summer thunderstorms come early."

"Lightning to the east," Dryden said.

"Heat, I think," Pike said. "But the sky is darkening, so who knows?"

Dryden was silent for a few moments, then said: "Remember the old days, Major? The war?"

"I remember."

"Good times," Dryden said.

Pike said: "Not for me. Leastways after I stepped in the way of a canister of Yankee grapeshot."

Dryden turned and looked at the younger man. "You know why I took you back to my headquarters that day?"

"You wanted your personal surgeon to operate on me."

"I told you that?"

"No, I guess not. But that's what I always figured."

"That wasn't the reason," Dryden said.

"Then I don't know why. Braver men than me were left to die of their wounds in the Wilderness."

"It was a question of counterweight, Major," Dryden said.

Pike shook his head. "Now you've lost me, General."

"I killed a lot of men in the war with my own hand," Dryden said. "And, whenever possible, I didn't take prisoners, so I stood by and watched the bayonet do for count-less others."

He stared at Pike. "You see it now, don't you? That saving your life would be the counterweight that provided a balance for all the lives I'd taken."

"It would help you with your guilt, you mean," Pike said.

"No, Charlie, not guilt," Dryden said. "I had none, not then and not now."

Pike smiled. "Then I'd say if I was your counterweight, the Yankees got the worst of the bargain."

"I'm seeking such balance again," Dryden said, as though he hadn't heard. "In Texas."

"By dying there?" Pike said.

"Yes. That's part of it. The cancer eats at me and soon I'll be forced to take the laudanum that Loretta brought with her."

Pike looked to the east. Lightning flashed in the distance and he heard a rumble of thunder. The wind was cool on his face.

"I'd better get a fire started," he said.

"Wait. Try to understand, Charlie," Dryden said. He thought a moment, then said: "All those years I spent on the bench, the law I brought to the north of this territory, where is the thanks, the appreciation?"

"I don't know," Pike said.

"When we left Breeze, was there a brass band?" Dryden said. "Was the mayor there in his sash of office, the city notables? Did they speechify, praising me for taming this part of the frontier?"

"No, I guess not," Pike said.

"No, you guess not," Dryden said. "And now that slight needs to be balanced. My journey to Texas will prove to be the counterweight, Charlie. Do you understand me now?"

Pike looked into Dryden's eyes. They were not mad, but they were on fire, the burning gaze of an Old Testament prophet.

He sought a way out. "I'll get you to Texas, Judge," he said. "Depend on it."

"Thank you, Charlie," Dryden said.

"Though I fear that will be but half the battle."

Loretta burst out of the trees. "Hey, Charlie," she said. "Make a fire, it's getting damned cold." She rubbed her butt. "All kinds of nettles back there."

CHAPTER 9

The sky flared with soundless lightning. A rising wind guttered the flames of the fire and kicked up showers of scarlet sparks.

"You're a good cook, Charlie," Loretta said.

Pike smiled. "Fried bacon and sourdough bread don't take much skill."

"I can't cook," Loretta said. She thought a moment, then said: "Wait, I can cook eggs. I fry them in butter and they're good if I don't break the yolks."

"Your talents don't lie in that direction, my dear," Dryden said.

The firelight glowed red on his face, the hollows of his cheeks and eyes in deep shadow. The wind raised a strand of his wispy black hair.

"Yeah, well, being a whore ain't easy either," Loretta said.

Pike built a cigarette and lit it with a brand from the fire. He glanced at the restless sky.

"Rain's holding off."

"Too early in the season for rain, Charlie," Dryden said.

"I reckon," Pike said.

"Hello the camp!"

Dryden stayed where he was, his forearms on his knees, but Pike rose to his feet. He scanned the windswept darkness where pine needles tumbled, then moved out of the firelight.

"Come on in, real open, like you was calling on kinfolk," Pike said.

"Got a banjo in my hands," the man's voice said. "Been tuning it. I reckon you should know."

Banjo . . . banjo . . . Pike racked his brain. Why did that ring an odd bell with him?

"Comin' on in," the man in the darkness said. "Riding me a bay hoss and I'm dragging along a pack mule."

The gloom parted and a fat man wearing a gray frock coat and a low-crowned hat of the same color rode into the lightning-streaked light. He had a banjo slung across his chest and he made no attempt to dismount.

"Howdy, folks," he said. "Name's Samuel Free. My friends call me Sam."

Now Pike got it and the realization chilled him to the bone.

"Smelled your coffee," Free said. His round face beamed.

"Then light and set," Dryden said. "We can always spare a cup."

"You stay right where you are, Free," Pike said.

The fat man's head turned to Pike, slowly, like a lizard. "You got a knot that needs untying, cowboy?" he said.

"I reckon so. Are you Banjo Sammy Free from down Gonzales County way?"

"There ain't likely to be two of us, now, is there?" Free said.

"You hung with Manny Clements and that hard bunch," Pike said.

"That was years ago," Free said. "Now I'm in business for myself."

Pike's eyes moved over the fat man. "Where's your Sharps?"

Free's features hardened. "I rode in for coffee, mister, not to answer questions."

"Yes, really, Charlie," Dryden said. "Is this completely necessary?"

"Where's your Sharps?" Pike said.

"Damn you, it's on the pack mule," Free said.

"Five hundred dollars is a lot of money in this territory," Pike said. "And in Texas, come to that."

"I don't know what the hell you're talking

about," Free said.

A stick fell in the fire, raising a shower of sparks.

"It's blood money, Sammy," Pike said. "The kind of money that brings the rats out of their holes. Bushwhacking rats like you."

Free slung the banjo onto his back. "I'm getting mighty sick o' you, cowboy," he said.

"We end it right here, Sammy," Pike said.

He drew and fired.

Free was a big man and he took the hit. But his eyes got wide and his flabby jaw dropped.

Pike fired again.

This time Free toppled off his horse. Frightened, the bay snorted and pulled away. Free's boot had caught in the stirrup and he was dragged into the night.

Dryden got to his feet.

"Why did you kill that man?" he demanded.

"Because he would have killed you, Judge," Pike said. "Somewhere between here and Texas, as surely as night follows day."

"He was a hired killer?"

"Banjo Sammy Free was one of the best, or worst, depending how you look at it," Pike said. "He used a Sharps fifty and he always hit what he aimed at. You don't take chances with a man like that."

"Then he was after —"

"Yeah, Clem Dredge's reward."

"You knew him?" Dryden asked.

"Heard of him," Pike said. "My *segundo* is forever talking about gunfighters, outlaws and sure-thing killers. Sammy Free's name was one he always mentioned."

"Then we had a lucky escape," Dryden said.

"I reckon. Manny Clements is no shrinking violet, but one time he told me that Free was the only man who ever scared him. Sammy's boast was that he'd cut any man, woman or child off at the knees with a shotgun for fifty dollars."

"How did he find us?" Dryden asked. He sounded worried.

"I don't think our whereabouts is a big secret, Judge," Pike said.

"I would like to have heard him play the banjo," Loretta said.

"Sammy always liked to do some pickin' after he killed a man," Pike said. "Said it relaxed him."

"Then screw him," Loretta said.

"I think Charlie already did, my dear," Dryden said.

"He could be lying wounded out there," Loretta said. "Should we take a look?"

"A wounded rattlesnake can still kill you," Pike said. "We'll wait until morning."

Pike sat by the fire and rolled another cigarette. Four men were already dead and the journey had only started. For the first time he began to wonder if Dryden's life was worth it.

CHAPTER 10

Sammy Free was dead when Pike found his body in the morning.

The man had sixty dollars in his wallet. Pike threw the wallet away and shoved the money in his pocket.

He was having second thoughts about Dryden, but that didn't mean he couldn't make a profit on this trip.

Pike shoved Free's Colt in his waistband and was about to turn his attention to the pack mule when Dryden and Loretta stepped beside him.

"I reckon a fat man would be well provided with grub," Pike said. "I'll take a look at the mule."

Dryden glanced at the body. "Two shots to the chest, not a handbreadth apart," he said. "Good shooting, Charlie."

"Like I said, you don't take a chance with men like him," Pike said.

Loretta gave a little squeal of delight.

"Ooh, look," she said, "lemon drops."

She had pulled a sack of candy from the mule's pack and was bouncing on her toes. "I love lemon drops," Loretta said, and popped one in her mouth.

Pike stepped beside her. He examined the pack. "Bacon, salt pork, coffee, flour and salt," he said. "And this."

He untied a brown leather case from the pack. Inside was a single-shot Sharps-Borchardt rifle. He showed it to Dryden.

"A fine rifle," Dryden said.

Pike nodded. "It can hit a man a fair piece away."

"How far?"

"Five hundred yards, maybe longer," Pike said. "Some say in the right hands it's good out to a thousand, but I don't know about that."

"Will you keep it, Charlie?" Dryden asked.

By way of answer, Pike smashed the walnut stock into pieces against a rock. He threw the shattered rifle away.

"It's done enough killing," he said to Dryden. "Kinda like the man who owned it."

When Pike and the others rode out, he led the bay and Dryden took the mule's lead rope.

Rather than cross Largo Canyon, Pike followed it southeast as it swung through the mesa country. Before noon they crossed a dry creek and were in high plateau country five miles south of Gonzales Mesa when Pike saw dust ahead of them.

He waved the others into a stand of mixed juniper and mahogany and drew rein. "Riders ahead of us," he said.

"Are they looking for the judge?" Loretta asked.

"Could be," Pike said.

Loretta had been noisily sucking on lemon candies since they'd left camp that morning and Pike was irritated almost beyond endurance.

"We'll stay right where we're at and let them come to us," he said. He looked around him. "There's cover here."

Dryden slid the Henry out from under his knee. He handled the heavy rifle effortlessly, a thing Pike noted.

Loretta spat out a candy. "We're all going to get killed before this is over," she said.

Pike said nothing, but Dryden grinned.

There was dappled shade among the trees, but the heat was intense, the sun hanging in the sky like a burning brass ball. Nowhere was there sound or movement, as though time had stopped and there was only now.

Pike watched the dust plume draw closer.

Dredge might have had these men keeping watch on the Old Spanish Trail and the San Pedro Mountains forty miles to the east. For some reason, boredom maybe, they'd decided to ride west in search of them.

Pike cursed his luck. Whether by accident or design, Dredge's gunmen were heading straight for them.

"What do you think, Charlie?" Dryden said.

"We'll dismount and take cover in the trees," Pike said.

"How many?"

"I don't know," Pike said. "Probably too many."

Dryden turned. "Loretta, climb down and —"

"Yeah, I heard. We're all dead anyway."

"They won't kill a woman," Pike said.

"Who told you that, Sir Galahad?" Loretta said. "Dredge's boys will put a bullet into me as cheerfully they would a man."

"It would be a great waste, my dear," Dryden said.

"If it comes to it, you tell them that, Henry," Loretta said.

Pike's gaze was fixed on the shimmering distance. "Let me have your glass, Judge."

He put the telescope to his eye, wiped

away beads of sweat with the back of his hand, then tried again.

"Five riders," Pike said.

"Are they likely lads?" Dryden said.

"I reckon," Pike said.

"They'll fight?"

"Depend on it."

"Then we'd better take up our positions," Dryden said.

"Wait," Pike said. "I see something."

He put the telescope to his eye again. Then: "What the hell . . . ?"

"What do you see, Charlie?" Loretta said. She had dismounted and was sitting at the base of a tree, her dress hitched up to her knees.

"It's four men, with a prisoner," Pike said.

Dryden turned his head. "Charlie, why would Dredge's men have a prisoner?"

"Because they're not his riders," Pike said. "They could be lawmen of some kind."

"In this wilderness?"

"Yeah, if they're a posse that's been on the scout for a spell."

"Then what do we do?" Dryden said.

"Stay here. Wait for them."

The four bearded riders led a paint with a roped-up man on its back. They were white men, but their prisoner had the black eyes and long hair of an Apache/Mexican breed.

Suspicious, when the riders saw Pike and the others they drew rein and their rifles quickly appeared.

"Identify yourselves," a man wearing a high-button gray suit said. "And no fancy moves."

Pike was about to answer, but Dryden rode forward a few yards and said pompously: "I am Judge Henry J. Dryden, late of the Federal Court for the Northern New Mexico Territory."

He waved a hand. "These are my associates, Major Charles Pike and Miss Loretta Lamont."

Suspicion lingered for a few moments on the face of the man in the suit; then his features cleared. "Hangin' Hank?"

Dryden looked stiff. "I believe that's what the criminal element calls me."

"No offense, Judge," the man said. "Didn't expect to meet you, or anybody else, come to that. Not all the way out here."

"We're bound for Texas, sir," Dryden said. "I will . . . retire there."

The man in the suit looked puzzled. "How come you ain't on the railroad riding the cushions or taking a stage, Judge?"

"I have a certain weakness in the lungs," Dryden said. "I felt, as did my associates, that a ride in the fresh air would do me good. A locomotive spews coal dust, you understand."

Before the man could answer, Dryden said: "You have the advantage of me, sir. I know neither your name nor position."

"Name's Haze Denson, Judge. I'm chairman of the Broken Neck Vigilante Peace Commission and the town undertaker. The men with me are" — he pointed to each — "John Bates, Uriah Simpson and Caleb Witherspoon."

Denson eased himself in the saddle. "Broken Neck is to the northeast of here, Judge, up Tank Mountain way." He thumbed over his shoulder. "We've been on this animal's trail for six days. Finally caught up with him in the San Pedro foothills back yonder."

"And his offense?"

"Offenses, Judge. Rape, murder, robbery, hoss-stealing and arson to name just a few."

"He's a sullen-looking brute," Dryden said.

"That he is," Denson said. "His name's Leon Delgado, a Mescalero and Mexican breed, and he's as bad as they come."

Denson was silent, thinking, for a moment; then he said: "Hey, Judge, I reckon you can do us a big favor."

"You only have to name it," Dryden said.

CHAPTER 11

"We were taking Delgado back to Broken Neck to give him a fair trial, then hang him," Denson said. "But we don't have a real judge in town, only the vigilante commission."

"I'm afraid I can't return with you to Broken Neck, Mr. Denson," Dryden said. "That is out of the question."

"No need for that. My idea is to try him right here, Judge," Denson said. "Then it's all legal and aboveboard, like."

"And it will save us the expense of feeding him," John Bates said. He was a hard-eyed man who spoke softly, in a thin whisper.

"I'm retired," Dryden said.

"Once a judge, always a judge," Denson said.

Dryden sat his horse in silence for a while, deep in thought.

Finally he said: "And why not? We'll find a place in the shade and set up court."

"Like old times, huh?" Pike said.

"Do I detect a note of disapproval in your tone, Charlie?"

"I saw a man hanged one time," Pike said. "It's a dirty business."

"It's the law," Dryden said.

Denson found a clearing in the trees and he and his vigilantes dismounted. Delgado, silent and scowling, showing bruises on his face, was made to stand a little way apart from the others.

Bates looked around him. "Hell, Haze, I don't see a tree limb strong enough to take a rope," he said.

"We passed a cottonwood a mile or so back," Denson said. "We'll hang him there."

"Ain't you boys rushing things?" Pike said. "The man hasn't even been tried yet."

"You one o' them kneelers, mister? Or maybe a Quaker?" Bates said.

"No, neither one."

"That's strange, the way you talk I took you fer one or t'other."

Dryden sat on a dead tree stump. "Mr. Denson, I appoint you prosecutor. Major Pike and the three men with you will act as the jury."

"What about me, Henry?" Loretta said.

"Women are not allowed to sit on a jury, my dear," Dryden said.

"But this isn't a real courtroom," Loretta said.

"Judge, let her sit on the jury," Denson said. "Her opinion is as good as anybody else's."

"Very well," Dryden said. "Loretta, sit with the others."

He looked at Denson. "This court is now in session. The case seems pretty cut-and-dried to me and I see no reason to prolong the proceedings. Mr. Delgado has a long history of crime and violence, but let us hear his latest transgressions."

"Judge, all we have is Denson's word for his past crimes," Pike said.

Dryden ignored that. "The latest charges, Mr. Denson."

"If it please the court —"

"Very good, Mr. Denson, very good indeed," Dryden said. "Proceed."

"Two weeks ago, Delgado was hired as a handyman helper by a married couple named Williams who owned a farm three miles from the town of Broken Neck. They had one son."

"I see," Dryden said. "Proceed."

"Well, Your Honor," Denson said, "six days ago, Delgado scattered Mr. Williams' brains with a section of logging wagon tongue. He then proceeded to rape Mrs.

Williams —"

"Fore and aft," Bates growled.

"Please, no interruptions," Dryden said. "Proceed with your testimony, Mr. Denson."

"Your Honor, after he was done with Mrs. Williams —"

"Satisfied his savage lust, you mean," Dryden said.

"Yeah, that's correct, Your Honor. Well, anyhow, after he was done he cut Mrs. Williams' throat. Then he stole a horse and lit a shuck."

"And how did you come to learn of this crime, Mr. Denson?" Dryden asked.

"The son, Joseph Williams, aged ten, hid from Delgado and later ran all the way to town to report the crime. He witnessed his father's murder, but mercifully not the rape of his mother. I organized a posse right away and we left in pursuit."

"Did you see the bodies?" Dryden asked.

"Yes, Your Honor. Mrs. Williams was lying on the marital bed, as naked as the day she was born, her throat cut from ear to ear. Mr. Williams lay next to a haystack, his head bashed in, weltering in his blood."

Dryden turned his head to Delgado. "You have heard the charges leveled against you, Mr. Delgado. How do you plead, guilty or not guilty?"

"You go to hell," Delgado snapped. He spat in Dryden's direction.

"You have the look of a vicious desperado, Mr. Delgado," Dryden said, "and I'm going to take your statement as a plea of guilty."

Now he looked at his jury.

"You have heard the evidence and your decision is obvious. Do you find the defendant, Leon Delgado, guilty or not guilty? Ladies first."

"Guilty," Loretta said. "Pervert."

Pike gave a guilty verdict along with the others. They were going to hang the man anyway. Better to make it unanimous and get it over with.

"Leon Delgado, do you have anything to say before I pronounce sentence?" Dryden said.

The man spat again. "Go to hell, you son of a bitch."

"Leon Delgado, I sentence you to be taken hence to a place of execution where you will be hanged by the neck until you are dead," Dryden intoned. "And may God have mercy on your doomed soul."

Bates jumped to his feet and roughly pushed and kicked Delgado toward his horse.

"The court will now adjourn to the place

of execution and see that justice is done," Dryden said. There was a profane light in his face.

"I'll pass," Pike said.

"The guilty must hang, Charlie," Dryden said.

"Maybe. But I saw a man hung before."

"You think I was wrong to sentence Delgado to death?"

"I'm not saying that, Judge. I just don't like hangings."

"Nor do I, Charlie. But justice has to be done and seen to be done."

"Then do it without me, Judge."

Dryden shrugged. He looked at Loretta. "How about you, my dear?"

"Count me in," Loretta said. "I never seen a man hung before."

"Then go enjoy," Pike said.

He felt sick.

Pike sat at the base of a tree and lit another cigarette. It had been half an hour, but Dryden and Loretta had not yet returned.

Men had a way of dragging out a hanging, as though they never wanted it to end. Prayers, hymn singing, more prayers. There was nothing like sending the condemned to hell in an odor of sanctity.

Through a cloud of blue smoke, he

watched the rider come.

He was an old-timer, dressed in buckskins, astride a gaunt mule.

The old man drew rein. "Howdy," he said.

Pike nodded.

"You ain't at the hanging back there?" the man asked.

Pike shook his head. "I got no liking for hangings."

"Well, can't say as I blame you. All that shit and piss running down. Turns a man's stomach."

"Where you headed?" Pike asked.

"I don't know. Somewhere I ain't been before, I reckon."

"Prospecting?"

"Some. I do a little trapping as well."

"There's coffee in the pot," Pike said.

"Don't care for any. I run out of Arbuckles' three years ago up on the Yellowstone and didn't taste a drop for six months. Never had a hankering for coffee since."

He shifted in the saddle. "Could use a smoke, though."

Pike rose and passed the old-timer tobacco and papers. He watched as the man built a cigarette, then let him light it from his own.

"Thank'ee," the old man said. "I've had the baccy hunger for a month, maybe longer."

"Keep the makings," Pike said. "I got more."

"Obliged."

"You ever run into a man by the name of Clem Dredge in your travels?" Pike said. "He's in the territory somewhere."

"Not personal, no. Heard tell of him real recent, though."

"What did you hear?"

"He killed a deputy marshal in Santa Fe, oh, 'bout three, four weeks ago. I heard he skinned it for Texas." The old man turned shrewd eyes on Pike. "He kin of your'n?"

"Don't know the man. But I've been told he's a ranny to avoid."

"That he is. Always on the prod an' good with a gun. An' the feller who rides with him, gunfighter by the name of Simpson, is pure pizen."

"I'll ride around them," Pike said.

"That would be my advice," the old man said.

He touched his hat. "Well, I'll be on my way. Thank'ee again for the baccy, young feller."

"Ride easy," Pike said.

The old man turned and said over his shoulder, "That's a hangin' posse back there an' now they got the taste fer it, I hope you got a bill of sale fer your hoss."

His laughter rang in the air like a death knell.

CHAPTER 12

"As long as I live, I never want to see anything like that again," Loretta said.

"Hanging a man is a bad business," Pike said.

"His neck wasn't broke," Loretta said. "Poor bastard strangled to death. His legs kicked. Then he shit himself."

Dryden smiled. "You need a drop to break a man's neck. There's no drop off the back of a horse."

"Somebody could have shot him, Henry."

"He was sentenced to hang for his crimes, my dear. Not death by firing squad."

Loretta looked at Pike. "Would you have shot him, Charlie?"

"No, I guess not."

"Damn it, I would," Loretta said. "If I'd had a gun."

"Then we would have hanged you, my dear," Dryden said.

Loretta looked shocked. "You're jesting,

right, Henry?"

"I never make jests about the doings of my court," Dryden said.

"I wish I'd never come on this trip," Loretta said.

"You can always turn back," Dryden said. "Just don't take possession of my house until I'm dead."

Loretta lifted her coffee cup and spoke over the rim. "I can't go back. I can only go on."

"Why?" Dryden said.

"I don't know why. Maybe I thought you needed me."

"When I need you, my dear, you'll be the first to know."

In the firelight, Dryden didn't look like a dying man. His thin body was tense, alert, like a hawk that's just sighted a dove. To Pike, everything about the man seemed abrupt, poised on the edge of violence.

Here, at their camp in the Badland Hills, suddenly he was once again Brigadier General Henry J. Dryden, scourge of the Yankees, the bringer of death.

"You seem to be feeling better tonight, Judge," Pike said, a probing comment.

"I do? Then it's an illusion. The cancer gives me no rest, but I bear the pain."

"You should get the laudanum from Loretta."

"What laudanum?" Loretta said. "I don't have any laudanum. If I had, I'd be taking it after what I witnessed today."

"Ah, I thought I asked you to bring it," Dryden said.

"We never had any laudanum, Henry," Loretta said. "What the hell are you talking about?"

"My mistake, my dear," Dryden said. "I thought I'd procured a bottle from Dr. Mullins."

Pike poured himself coffee, thinking.

Dryden had lied about the laudanum. Maybe he was also lying about the cancer. Maybe he was lying about everything.

The question still remained: Why?

"Which way will you lead us, Charlie?" Dryden asked.

Pike took time to build a cigarette, then: "I figure to turn east just north of Santa Fe. We'll follow the Canadian, then ride south until we meet up with the Goodnight-Loving Trail. We can cross into Texas just north of the Pecos."

"As good a road as any, I suppose," Dryden said.

He was quiet for a moment, then said: "So, the old prospector told you Dredge is

89

in Texas."

"That's what he claimed," Pike said.

"I have friends in Texas," Dryden said. "We'll be safe there."

"By all accounts Dredge is a resourceful man," Pike said.

"We'll see," Dryden said.

"You still want to go to Waco?"

"That's where my friends are."

"I have reasons to get back to my ranch," Pike said. "One of them is that my lady friend may be with child."

"She tell you that, Charlie?" Loretta asked. All of a sudden she was looking at him with the hard, calculating eyes of a whore.

"Yes, she did."

"How late is she?"

"When I left? Two weeks."

Loretta laughed. "Hell, Charlie, I'm that late most of the time." She took a burning stick from the fire and poked it in his direction. "The bitch wants a husband."

"What's the lady's name?" Dryden asked.

"Maxine."

"Pretty name."

"Hey, Charlie, I bet ol' Maxine's been getting somebody else to poke her so she'll be well knocked up by the time you get back," Loretta said, grinning.

"Please, Loretta, the lady might well be enceinte already and I have no doubt that Charlie is the father," Dryden said.

"Time will tell," Loretta said.

Pike lay in his blankets beside the fire, his head on his saddle. He was enjoying his last cigarette of the day, watching the blue smoke haze the stars.

Loretta stepped out of the darkness and kneeled beside him.

"How's the judge?" Pike asked.

"Asleep. I guess the hanging wore him out."

"What's on your mind, Loretta?"

"A lot."

"Is that why you're here?"

"Yeah."

"You going to tell me about it?"

"I want you to take me to Santa Fe, Charlie. Leave me there, then go on to Texas."

Pike turned his head. "Why Santa Fe?"

"I can work in a house there."

"What about the judge?"

"What about him?"

"He needs you, Loretta."

"That's a laugh, Charlie. There was a time he needed me in his bed. Now there's not even that. He hasn't come near me in months. Hell, even the bite marks he left on my tits healed long ago."

Pike took a last draw of his cigarette, lifted his head and tossed the butt in the fire. "You could go back to Breeze, live in the judge's house."

"Henry won't let me live there. He has no intention of giving me his home. Maybe he plans on going back one day."

"He's dying, Lorraine."

"He says he's dying."

"Is he, or isn't he?"

"I don't know."

"Why would he lie about it?"

"I don't know that either."

Lorraine stared into the fire; then she said, blinking, "He does need you, Charlie."

"I know. He needs me to get him to Texas with his hide intact."

He rose to a sitting position. "And that leads to another question: Why me? He could have hired a couple of guns in Breeze who would see him safely home."

"He doesn't trust anyone, Charlie," Loretta said. "You are the only exception."

"Because I wore the gray? Because he saved my life?"

"I don't know, Charlie."

She rose to her feet. "Will you take me to Santa Fe?"

"I'll talk to the judge."

"Screw him. If he says no, I'll go on my own."

"And what will you do for a horse, my dear? The paint you ride is mine."

Dryden stood like an alabaster pillar, his thin body tinged scarlet by the firelight. He held a riding crop in his right fist.

CHAPTER 13

"What did you say to Charlie, Loretta?" Dryden asked.

The woman looked scared. "I said I'd go to Santa Fe on my own, Henry. I didn't mean it."

"Before that, my dear. You said two words. What were they?"

"I don't remember."

"Ah, but you do. Repeat them, my dear." Dryden ground his teeth. "Repeat them, you bitch."

"Please, Henry, I —"

"Repeat them!"

"I said, 'Screw him.' Please, I was only joking."

"Vile words from the filthy mouth of a whore," Dryden said. "You must be punished for them, my dear." He smiled. "Remove your clothes at once."

"No, please, Henry, don't whip me," Loretta said, shrinking away from the man.

94

"Yes, my dear, the whip," Dryden said. "Then Charlie and I will both take you again and again until we're glutted. We'll hurt you badly, Loretta. Depend on it."

Pike slammed on his hat and rose to his feet. He was holding his gun.

"Back off, Judge," he said. "Leave the woman alone."

Dryden's eyes glittered. "Are you taking her side, Charlie?"

"There are no sides," Pike said. "Loretta cusses all the time and she said something she regrets. Now let it go. I won't see a woman abused. I saw it happen to my mother when I was a boy. I won't stand for it now I'm a man."

"She must be punished, Charlie." Dryden stared at Loretta. "Strip. I want you naked in your shame."

"Judge!"

The triple click of the Colt hammer being thumbed back was loud in the quiet.

"Will you shoot me, Charlie?" Dryden said.

"If I have to," Pike said.

"She said vile words, Charlie. She must suffer the consequences."

"Screw you, Henry," Pike said.

"Et tu, Brute?" Dryden said.

"Yeah, I said it. Now, if you have a mind

to lay on with that whip, have at it."

Dryden looked at the gun steady in Pike's hand, then said to Loretta. "Very well, my dear, we'll find a hog ranch in Santa Fe for you, as you desire. After all, it's the only thing that's left to you."

He stared at Charlie. "Would you have pulled the trigger?"

"You'll never know, Judge," Pike said. "Like you, I'm a man of mystery."

"I'm dying, Charlie. Death is the only mystery left to me," Dryden said.

The aspens on the slopes of the nearby Sangre de Cristo Mountains were trembling in a gusting wind as Pike and the others rode into the bustling adobe city of Santa Fe.

Veils of dust lifted from the streets and the wind set the shutters of the earth-colored buildings to banging. People walked with their faces covered against driving sand, their heads bent.

Pike lifted his bandana over his mouth and nose, leaving only his red eyes clear, and Loretta tried to shelter behind her fluttering parasol.

Only Dryden seemed immune from wind and dust, sitting erect in his saddle, his still face like a graven image, a steel veil covering his eyes.

As they rode past a large church, Loretta stopped an old woman in the street and shouted against the keening wind: *"Señora, cual es el nombre de esa iglesia?"*

The woman hurriedly crossed herself. *"Es la Catedral de San Francisco de Asis."*

Loretta thanked the woman and drew rein. "Charlie, I'm going into the church."

Pike tugged down his bandana. "What church?"

Loretta pointed. "There. The Cathedral of Saint Francis of Assisi."

"Why?"

"To pray for my soul and yours. And Henry's."

Dryden rode back. He took in what was happening at a glance.

"My dear, that's a church, not a whore-house," he said.

"I know, Henry," Loretta said. "I'm going inside to pray for you."

"Pray for yourself, my dear," Dryden said. "Your need is greater than mine." He made a motion with his hand. "Climb down. I want my horse."

"Let her keep the horse until she's settled," Pike said. The wind flattened his hat brim against the front of the crown.

"I don't trust a two-dollar whore to return a two-hundred-dollar paint," Dryden said.

"Climb down, Loretta."

"I don't want his horse, Charlie," Loretta said. She stepped out of the saddle and handed Pike the reins.

Looking up at him, she said: "Be careful, Charlie. I think you're riding into terrible danger."

Before Pike could answer, she turned on her heel and walked away. But after a dozen steps she turned and yelled: "And make an honest woman out of Maxine."

The two men watched Loretta leave, the lewd wind molding her skirts against her legs.

Dryden smiled. "Just what Santa Fe needs, another whore in church."

He looked at Pike. "Well, Charlie, I don't know about you, but I'm looking forward to a good supper and a soft bed tonight. I need rest, so shall we find a hotel and linger for a day or so?"

"Judge, I think you went hard on Loretta," Pike said. "In her own way, she is fond of you."

Dryden shook his head. "Charlie, she's a cheap whore. A man uses a woman like that until he tires of her. Then he tosses her aside."

He smiled like a death's-head. "Come, now, no more talk of whores. Let us find a hotel and enjoy the amenities of civilization for a few days."

Pike watched Loretta open the cathedral door.

Above her head, the soaring church loomed large and significant. But Loretta looked very small. And not significant at all.

CHAPTER 14

"Sure I seen it," the bartender said. "Didn't I see it with my own two eyes?"

"Where did it happen?" Pike said.

"The San Jacinto Billiard Room."

Pike tried his bourbon. It was smooth and good, backed by a foaming stein of Schlitz beer.

"See, Clem Dredge was playing eight ball with Luke Dandridge," the bartender said. "And —"

"I used to like that game," Dryden said. He turned to the pretty young woman who was with him. "Did you ever play, Suzette?"

"Tried it once," Suzette said. "My tits kept getting in the way of the stick."

"I can understand that, my dear," Dryden said.

The bartender seemed slightly irritated that his story had been interrupted.

"Well, anyhoo," he said, "Luke was one of the town's deputy marshals and he tended to be a quick-tempered man, especially in drink. He won the game fair and square and told Dredge that he owed him fifty cents.

"Dredge says, 'The hell I do, the bet was for best out of three.'

"Both of them had been drinking and Luke was getting madder by the minute. 'I know what the bet was,' he said. 'It was fifty cents a game.' "

Dryden smiled. "Seems like a piddling amount of money to upset a man so."

"Mister," the bartender said, "fifty cents is a day's wages around these parts."

Pike wiped beer foam off his mustache with the back of his hand.

"And then what happened?"

"Luke says, 'Damn you, Clem, are you going to pay me my due?'

"And Dredge says, 'Luke, you go to hell.'

"And Luke says, 'I have friends here and I won't be cheated this way.'

"Then somebody near me said, 'Here, this won't do.'

"Well, Dredge puts his hand inside his coat and Luke says, 'Don't go for your gun, Clem.'

"Then Luke made the last mistake of his life."

"He went for his own gun," Pike said.

"That's right, mister," the bartender said.

"Luke reached for the Colt in his scabbard, but Dredge drew from his waistband and put three bullets into him before he hit the floor.

"Then Dredge looked down at the body for a long time. Then he looked at the rest of us and said, 'Damn it all, boys, he was right. I did say fifty cents a game.' "

"Welching on a bet or no, it seems like a clear-cut case of self-defense to me," Dryden said.

The bartender wiped the area in front of Pike with a rag. "Maybe so, but the town didn't see it that way. Luke Dandridge was well liked when he was sober and there was hard talk coming down against Dredge, hanging talk. That's why he skipped."

"And now he's in Texas," Pike said.

"That's the word," the bartender said. "Some say he's in El Paso, others claim he's down Waco way. Who knows?"

The man left to serve a customer farther down the bar and Dryden said: "It's getting late. Charlie. I guess Suzette and I will turn in."

"Early start tomorrow, Judge," Pike said.

"I know. But I feel much better for the rest I got this past couple of days," Dryden said. He looked at Pike. "Are you calling it a night?"

"I figure I'll walk around the plaza for a spell," Pike said. "Get some fresh air."

"Then I'll say good night," Dryden said. "I'll meet you in the dining room for breakfast."

The plaza was thronged with promenading people and vendors of all kinds, the festive scene lit by lamps in the trees and a bright moon that hung in the lilac sky.

Pike lit a cigar he'd bought in the bar and strolled among the crowds, enjoying the lively talk and the beautiful, dark-eyed women.

Then he saw Loretta.

She was wearing a dress that was two sizes too large for her, but her blond hair and slight form were unmistakable.

Pike watched her walk up to a tall man, say something to him, only to have him laugh and walk away. She tried soliciting with another man, with the same result, only this time there was a scowl, not a laugh.

Pike walked closer to her and she turned to him, smiled and said: "Need company tonight, mister?" Then she put her hand over her mouth and said: "Oh!"

"Evening, Loretta," Pike said, touching his hat brim.

"I . . . I didn't recognize you," Loretta said.

Pike smiled. "Amazing what a shave and a haircut can do for a man, even one as downright homely as me."

She looked over his shoulder. "Where's Henry?"

"Asleep, I reckon. We're heading out in the morning."

The left side of Loretta's face had been in shadow, but now her features were visible in the moonlight.

"What happened to you?" Pike said.

Loretta's left eye was so badly injured it was grotesque, swollen shut, the surrounding skin black and blue, tinged with mustard yellow.

"Nothing," she said. "It's nothing."

"Who did that to you?" Pike said.

He did not particularly like Loretta, but they shared a common bond in Dryden and in a way, strange even to himself, he felt responsible for her.

"I asked you who did this, Loretta," Pike said.

"I need a drink, Charlie."

"There's a cantina near the hotel. We'll go there."

Pike watched Loretta down a shot of mescal, then filled her glass from the bottle on the table.

"Tell me about it," he said. A slow anger was growing in him. In the cantina's hard lamplight, Loretta's eye looked much worse.

"His name is Jacob Milner and he owns a house on Santo Marco Street," Loretta said. "He told me I could work in the house on a fifty-fifty split."

She lifted her glass and Pike refilled it.

"My first night, I made eight dollars," Loretta said. "Milner took seven and when I objected he beat me up and threw me out. He enjoys beating whores, kinda like Henry."

She smiled. "I'm broke, I've got nowhere to live and looking like this, no man will come near me. There's a sad tale to tell your little schoolteacher, huh, Charlie?"

"Drink up," Pike said. "We're leaving."

"Leaving for where?"

"I'm going to talk to good ol' Jacob. I want your money back and another fifty for the damage to your eye."

"Charlie, he's big. He's much bigger than you and he's tough."

"A man who beats up women isn't tough," Pike said. "Let's go."

"Forget it, Charlie," Loretta said. "I'm a

105

whore. It goes with the territory."

"Not where I come from," Pike said.

CHAPTER 15

Santo Marco Street lay only a short distance from the plaza. Milner's house was unusual in that it was one of the few two-story buildings in Santa Fe.

A sign over the door read:

THE HORNY ROOSTER
A Gentlemen's Club

Pike stepped inside, into a foyer. A staircase lay directly ahead of him, corridors on both sides leading to rooms. From behind a closed door to his right, an iron cot squealed, the whore in the bed squealing even louder.

"Where can I find Milner?" Pike said.

"Please, Charlie, don't," Loretta said. "He'll kill you."

"Where is he?"

"The room there, to the left of the stairs. He usually has a girl with him."

Pike looked around him. A statue of a naked lady with no arms stood on a console table. The statue was about two feet tall, made of plaster and the base was square and heavy.

Pike picked up the statue and liked the heft. He grabbed the lady by her head and hid her behind his back as he stepped to Milner's door.

He pointed to Loretta, then made a yapping mouth of his fingers and thumb.

The woman nodded and Pike rapped on the door.

"Beat it, I'm busy." A man's harsh voice from inside.

"Jacob, it's me, Loretta. I've come back."

"I'll deal with you later, bitch," Milner said. "Now get lost."

Pike grinned and rapped on the door again, this time louder.

There was no answer and Pike heard the rhythmic cranking of the bed.

Now he kicked at the door hard with his booted right foot.

There was a bellow from inside.

"I'm gonna beat the crap out of you, bitch!" Milner roared.

Loretta suddenly looked scared.

Pike heard bare feet thud on carpet. He held the statue in both hands, the heavy base pointed downward.

The door swung open and a thickset man with a bullet head and no neck stood in the doorway. His jaw dropped when he saw Pike.

"What the hell!"

Milner didn't get a chance to say anything else. He opened his mouth to talk, but Pike, driving hard, filled it with the base of *Venus de Milo.*

The blow staggered Milner. He lurched back into the room on rubber legs, spitting blood and teeth.

Pike knew the man would be a handful and he didn't give him a chance to set. He swung the statue and this time the base caught Milner on the left side of his head.

The man reeled, tripped on the upturned rug and fell onto his hands and knees.

Pike drew back his leg and kicked Milner in the face. The pimp groaned and rolled over on his back, his entire head a mass of blood.

"Good evening, Jake," Pike said. "Sorry to call on you this late."

He glanced over to the naked woman in the bed. She was smiling and made no attempt to cover her breasts with the sheet.

Pike touched his hat. "Evening, ma'am."

Milner tried to get to his feet, failed and

propped his elbow on the seat of a chair. "Who are you?" he said. Blood from his mouth ran over his hairy chest and Pike's kick had broken his nose and closed one of his eyes. "What the hell do you want?"

The statue had broken off at the base and Pike held it up to Milner. "Sorry about the statue, Jake, but you've got a hard head."

Milner turned. "Annie, get the damned town marshal."

"I wouldn't do that, Annie," Pike said. "Jake and me are about to have a business meeting and I don't want any interruptions."

Annie shrugged and stayed where she was.

"You ready to dicker, Jake?" Pike said.

"Dicker about what, damn you?"

"Well, for a start, about the seven dollars you owe Miss Lamont."

Milner's tongue moved in his mouth; then he spat out a piece of tooth.

"The whore can have her seven dollars," he said.

"Then there are damages," Pike said. "Compensation for the injury to Miss Lamont's eye."

"Look at me!" Milner yelled. "Look what you did to me, you bastard. I need compensation."

"So, we want the seven dollars and, say,

fifty for the black eye," Pike said. "Oh, why quibble, Jake? Let's call it a hundred even."

"I'm not giving a whore a hundred dollars," Milner said.

"Then I'm going to hurt you again, Jake," Pike said.

"No!" Milner yelled. "All right, damn you, the writing is on the wall and I can read it plain. You're a shakedown artist. I get it now."

He rose painfully to his feet.

"I keep my money in the dresser," he said.

"Then go get it, Jake," Pike said.

Milner staggered to the dresser and opened a top drawer.

Pike pulled his Colt from his waistband and thumbed back the hammer.

"All I want to see in your hand is money," he said. "If you come up with a gun, I'll be very cross with you."

Milner stood still, looking into the drawer, thinking things through.

Finally he pulled out a wad of notes and slammed the drawer shut.

"Give the money to Miss Lamont," Pike said.

"All of it?" Milner said.

"All of it."

"There's five hundred dollars here," Milner said.

"I think she deserves it, don't you?" Pike said.

The muzzle of the Colt dropped until it was level with Milner's belly.

"All of it, Jake."

Loretta stepped close to the man and extended her left hand.

Milner slapped the money into her palm. "Take it, bitch and be damned to ye."

Loretta's knee came up fast into Milner's groin. The big man's eyes popped and he clutched at himself. He sank slowly to the floor, his bloody face purple.

"Serves you right," Loretta said. "That's what you get for striking a lady."

Pike glanced at the woman on the bed. "Sorry, looks like ol' Jake isn't going to be much use to you for a spell."

"He wasn't much use to me before she broke his balls," the woman said.

"Let's go, Loretta," Pike said.

Milner fought through his pain and managed to talk. "Mister," he said, "I'm going to remember you. I'm going to remember you real good."

There were a hundred kinds of death in the man's eyes.

"And I'll always remember you, Jake," Pike said. "Especially your boundless generosity toward the poor and oppressed."

CHAPTER 16

"You'll have to leave Santa Fe, Loretta," Pike said. "I don't think Jake is a man to forgive and forget."

"Five hundred dollars will help me cover a lot of ground," Loretta said. "And I've got you to thank for it, Charlie."

"I don't like to see women or children abused," Pike said. "I never did."

The crowds had thinned out at the plaza as he led Loretta in the direction of the hotel.

"You don't like me much, do you, Charlie?" Loretta said.

"Like you say, not much."

"Why?"

"I guess you're not my idea of what a woman should be."

"What should she be?"

"I don't know. A ranch wife, I guess."

"Skin like saddle leather by the time she's forty, old and bent from hard work at fifty?

Is that your ideal woman?"

"I didn't say that."

"You said a ranch wife. I told you what happens to them. I saw it happen to my mother."

"Well, it won't happen to my wife," Pike said.

"How are you going to manage that, living on a one-loop spread?"

"I don't know."

"You don't know what?"

"How I'll manage it."

"You could lock her away in a room, Charlie. Keep the sun off her and let her get good and fat."

Pike stopped. "One thing I do know, Loretta."

"What's that?"

"I'll never marry you. I swear you'd nag a man to death."

"Don't worry about it, Charlie, you're not my type."

Loretta was silent for a moment, then said: "Strange you fought for the South, Charlie."

"What's so strange about it?"

"You've got such a long, Yankee face, like you never laughed in your life."

Pike stopped. "Loretta, you've got a strange way of thanking a man for what he just did for you."

"I already thanked you. I said I'm beholden to you for the five hundred dollars. What more do you want?"

"Nothing. I guess you've thanked me enough."

They walked on and a silence stretched between them.

Then Loretta said: "I like you, Charlie. And you're fun to tease because you're such a mope."

"Well, Loretta, you can mope on this: The hotel is full because some kind of spring fiesta starts tomorrow."

"That's all right, Charlie, I was planning to sleep in your bed tonight anyway," Loretta said.

"With me?"

"No, not with you."

"Then where will I sleep?"

"On the floor."

Pike shook his head. "You won't try to kill me in my sleep, huh?"

Loretta smiled. "You never can tell, Charlie boy."

Dryden was halfway through breakfast when Pike and Loretta stepped into the dining room. There was no sign of Suzette.

If Dryden was surprised he hid it well.

He rose to his feet, smiling. "Why, Loretta, how nice to see you again."

Looking from the woman to Pike, Dryden said: "Did you have a pleasant night?"

"She did. I didn't," Pike said. "She slept on the bed and I slept on the rug. That's why I'm stiff and sore this morning and more than a mite irritable."

Dryden sat. "How disappointing. I was expecting more."

"That's it, Judge," Pike said. "There's nothing more."

He looked around. "Where's Suzette?"

"Gone. She left this morning."

"Suzette, huh?" Loretta said. "You're hiring a better class of whore, Henry."

"That would not be too difficult, my dear," Dryden said. He stared at Pike. "Why?"

"We have to take her with us, Judge."

"Why?"

"Well, the black eye is obvious," Pike said.

"And the rest of the story?" Dryden said.

Pike told him.

Dryden waited until the waiter poured coffee for Pike and Loretta; then he said: "This Jacob Milner, is he a vindictive man?"

"Judge, I beat him up with a statue and then Loretta pulverized his balls," Pike said. "Wouldn't that make any man vindictive?"

"Yes," Dryden said, "I suppose it would."

"We'll watch our back trail," Pike said.

"You've put this entire expedition in jeopardy, Charlie. You know that, don't you?" Dryden said.

"I had no choice."

"Ah yes, the knight errant riding to the rescue of a" — he looked at Loretta's eye — "not so fair maiden."

Dryden dabbed his lips with his napkin. "Very well, then, what's done is done. Drink up your coffee, both of you. We better ride and put distance between us and Milner."

"I haven't had breakfast yet," Lorraine said.

"You and Charlie are late. There's no time for breakfast."

Dryden got to his feet. "Loretta, you can come with us until we cross into Texas. Then I'm done with you."

"The feeling is mutual, Henry," Loretta said.

CHAPTER 17

For three days Pike rode southwest, keeping the Canadian in sight, then swung due south to join up with the Goodnight-Loving Trail.

Along the way they switched the supplies to Dryden's horse and let Free's balky mule go.

By nature Pike was not a talking man, but he did his best to fill the void of silence that stretched between Dryden and Loretta by jawing about everything and anything.

But when the bacon ran out and they began to reuse coffee grounds, the dead air grew more hostile and it was with some relief that Pike led the way into Fort Sumner on the Pecos.

They bought coffee, salt pork, flour, dried apples and sourdough starter at Pete Maxwell's place, then rode south again.

When the four-thousand-foot peak of Dipping Vat Hill loomed in the distance, their troubles finally caught up with them.

"Rider on our back trail," Pike said.

Dryden turned in the saddle. "I don't see him."

"He's there, among the cottonwoods by the creek," Pike said. "He's got a glass."

"Dredge?" Dryden asked.

"Could be, but my money's on Jake Milner," Pike said. "He didn't strike me as a forgetful ranny. I guess he wants his five hundred back."

"And me," Loretta said.

"And both of us," Pike said.

He looked behind him. "I'm not a far-seeing man, but I reckon there's now four of them. Can you make them out, Loretta?"

Loretta swung her paint around.

"I'd swear the one in the black frock coat is Milner," she said. "He's standing in the stirrups, watching us with the glass."

Pike smiled. "After what you did to him, he'll be standing all right. The others?"

Loretta shook her head. "Just three big men, probably Santa Fe toughs."

"Then I'm off the hook," Dryden said. "They're not after me."

"Hell, Judge, you're riding for the brand," Pike said.

A Western man born and bred, disloyalty was a thing Pike had never experienced and did not understand.

"It's your fight, Charlie," Dryden said, "not mine. I won't endanger my life needlessly."

"You're dying anyway, Henry," Loretta said.

"And I'll choose the manner of my death," Dryden said. "Getting killed in a brawl with a whoremaster over one of his women is not what I choose."

"If it comes to a fight, I'm going to need your gun skill," Pike said.

"Charlie, I told you, it's your fight, not mine. Deal with it."

Dryden touched his hat. "I'll bid you both good day."

"Henry, you son of a bitch, there's four of them," Loretta said.

"And therein lies your problem," Dryden said.

He raked his spurs across his horse's belly and rode away at a gallop. A shifting ribbon of dust marked his passing.

"He's yellow," Loretta said. "A damned coward."

Pike shook his head. "Dryden is not a coward, Loretta. He's far from being yellow."

"Then why the hell did he run out on us?"

"He wants to stay alive."

"Why?"

"I wish I knew."

Loretta cast a fearful glance at the riders among the cottonwoods.

"Can we outrun them, Charlie?" she said.

"Maybe, for a while," Pike said. "But we'll have to face them sooner or later. If that is Milner, he's a determined man and a cautious one. He's taking his time, making sure we're alone."

"We're neck deep in shit, ain't we, Charlie?" Loretta said.

"Seems like."

Pike studied the rolling land ahead of him.

"What do you see?" Loretta asked.

"Nothing. Miles of nothing."

"Then what do we do?"

"Light a shuck." Pike gathered the reins. "You ready?"

Loretta nodded.

"Then let's go," Pike said.

He kneed the big sorrel into a run, Loretta close behind him.

"They're coming, Charlie," she said.

"Figured they would."

Shouting over the pounding of hooves and the rush of the wind, Loretta said: "You better come up with a real good idea, Charlie. Those boys behind us aren't about to let us go."

Pike turned his head. "I don't have any ideas."

"Oh, great," Loretta said.

Dipping Vat Hill was close when the men behind Pike and Loretta began firing probing shots, splitting the air close to them.

"They're gaining on us, Charlie," Loretta said.

"Seems like."

Milner, if that was who he was, and his men had fresher horses and they were steadily making ground. The chase was becoming close and dangerous.

Pike spared a quick glance for their pursuers, then turned in the saddle. "Loretta, make for the oaks over yonder to the left of the hill."

"You're going to get us killed, Charlie," Loretta said.

"Damn it, woman, do as I say."

"All I see is two trees and a rock," Loretta said.

"I know," Pike said. "But it's all we got. Now go."

Loretta swung her pony toward the trees, churning up veils of yellow dust.

Pike slid the Winchester out from under his knee and levered a round into the chamber.

He looked behind him.

This was going to be close. He had five seconds at most to swing out of the saddle and start firing.

He was cutting it fine. Maybe too fine.

Loretta, cursing like a madwoman, rode past the oaks, trying to fight her wild-eyed paint to a halt.

Pike drew rein, jumped out of the saddle and fetched himself up against one of the trees. He threw the Winchester to his shoulder and dusted three fast shots at the man in the frock coat.

Pike was counting on the man being Milner. More, he was staking his life on it.

He scored no hits, but as he'd hoped, Frock Coat did not come on. He broke to his left, then galloped away. The three men with him milled around for a moment, then followed.

Feeding shells into his rifle, he watched Milner — he was now sure it was the big pimp — and his boys draw off a couple of hundred yards and stop.

They started to argue among themselves and Pike smiled.

He had pegged Milner as a woman beater, a man with no real bottom to him, all threat and bluster. The man was a coward and charging into a Winchester was obviously not something in which he took any pleasure.

He'd do well enough as a bushwhacker, a sure-thing artist, but coming up against a tough and determined man had unnerved him.

The next move was Milner's.

And it was not long in coming.

Milner rode closer, stood in the stirrups and yelled: "Hey, cowboy, can you hear me?"

"I can hear you."

"Give me the woman and my five hundred dollars and you can ride clear," Milner said.

"Go to hell, Jake."

"Cowboy, I'm willing to let bygones be bygones," Milner said. "No use crying over spilled milk, I say."

Pike made no answer.

Milner said: "The whore means nothing to you. Let me have her and the money."

"Hey, Jake," Pike said, "how are your balls?"

Milner threw his rifle to his shoulder and fired a wild shot. "Cowboy," he said as the echoes drifted away, "your big mouth just talked you into a bullet."

CHAPTER 18

Loretta dropped beside Pike. "Damn horse," she said.

"What happened?"

"He ran away with me, little son of a bitch," Loretta said.

"Well, you're here, so you got him stopped."

"Eventually."

"Thanks for coming back," Pike said.

She looked at him and smiled. "I ride for the brand, Charlie."

Loretta scanned the land around her, her eyes resting on the four men. They had dismounted and were sitting in a circle talking, holding on to the reins of their horses.

"Is it Milner?" she asked.

"Uh-huh."

"I heard shooting. Did you get him?"

"Nope. I dusted around him a little and he skedaddled."

"He won't fight."

"He won't stand and fight. He'll try something sneaky."

"Come dark, maybe?"

"That would be my guess."

"You should have shot him, Charlie."

"I was trying my best. I never was much of a hand with a rifle, except close up."

Pike looked at Loretta. "Dryden took off with all the supplies."

"That sounds like him," Loretta said.

"I could sure use some coffee," Pike said.

"Charlie, would you really start a fire and bile coffee with Milner and his boys so close?"

"Why not? We've got some time before dark. Milner isn't going to come at me in the daylight. He learned that lesson, ol' Jake did."

Loretta watched Pike build and light a cigarette.

"What do we do when it gets dark, Charlie?" she asked.

"I'm studying on it," Pike said.

Loretta looked at the sky. "Study on it hard, Charlie. It will be dark soon enough."

"I have to scare Jake," Pike said. "He's the weak link in the chain. Scare him bad enough and he'll scamper."

"What does he want from us?" Loretta said. "All this just to kill us?"

"He told me what he wants."

"He did?"

"Sure enough. He wants you and the five hundred. Said I could ride free if I gave you to them."

"What did you say?"

"I said, 'Sure, as soon as her horse stops, you can have the bitch.'"

"You wouldn't say that, Charlie. You're laced too tight for that."

Pike smiled. "I told him to go to hell. Then I asked him how his balls were holding up."

"What did he say?"

"He fired his rifle at me, so I guess they're still hurting something fierce."

Loretta laughed. She had white teeth in a pink mouth and Pike thought it a good sound to hear. Rough living and foul-mouthed though she was, the lady had backbone.

An hour passed and shadows were gathering on the barren slopes of Baldy Mountain, three miles to the southwest. Normally the peak was swarming with gold miners, but the army had ordered them out for the duration of the Geronimo scare.

To the east, the setting sun made the flat top of Table Mountain shine like a twenty-dollar coin, a promise of gold as illusionary as a fairy gift.

127

"How are you going to play this, Charlie?" Loretta said.

"I don't know," Pike said.

"You mean we're dead?"

"I mean, I don't know."

"Then think of something, fast."

"I have to get to Jake," Pike said. "He's a slender reed."

"Then walk out there and shoot the son of a bitch," Loretta said.

"Not much future in that," Pike said. "The three with him don't look like pushovers. They'd plug me for sure."

Loretta sighed. "It's almost dark. Do something, Charlie."

She tilted her head. "Hear that? The coyotes are coming for us."

Pike's mouth was dry and his belly was tying itself in knots.

He drew his Colt and passed it to Loretta. Then his rifle.

His eyes sought Loretta's in the gathering gloom.

"Listen up good. If I should fall, get on my horse and" — he pointed to the east — "ride thataway. The sorrel will take you where you need to go."

"What are you intending, Charlie?"

"I'm going after Jake."

Pike reached into his pocket, took out his

clasp knife and tested the blade with his thumb. "Blunt. But Jake doesn't know that."

He looked at Loretta. "Can you use that Winchester?"

"Hell, everybody can shoot a Winchester."

"You're a woman."

"Nice of you to notice, Charlie. But I can still shoot a Winchester."

Pike looked at the sky where the night birds were pecking at the first stars. The wind carried the scent of pines from distant blue mountains and spread it around like incense from an altar.

Now that he'd decided on a course of action, Pike's forehead was unwrinkled by thought or worry. It was near full dark and he had it to do.

"I'm going to sneak up on Jake, if I can," Pike said.

"I never took you for a man who would be good at sneaking up on people," Loretta said.

"Years of dodging Yankee pickets taught me how to sneak," Pike said. "By the end of the war, I got real good at it."

He nodded to Loretta. "Well, wish me luck."

Without another word, Pike bellied away from the rock and soon shrouded himself in darkness.

Behind him, Loretta whispered softly: "For God's sake be careful, Charlie."

The knife in his right hand, Pike crawled for twenty yards, then stopped, listening into the night. Coyotes yipped in the hills and the wind rustled the shrubs and bunchgrass.

There was no sign or sound of Milner and his men.

Pike began to crawl again. He covered another twenty yards, then stopped. To his surprise he smelled wood smoke.

Pike wondered at that. Could Jake be even more stupid than he originally thought?

He lifted his head and searched the darkness.

There! Ahead of him — the blush of firelight on the leaf canopies of a thicket of shinnery oak.

So Jake was just as stupid as he figured. He was getting prepared for a gunfight by building himself a fire.

Moving slowly, mindful of the whispering sound of his passing, Pike edged closer. The oaks grew behind a low rise and had been hidden from him until now. Milner and his boys had built their fire near the trees, where wood was handy.

Pike could see the men well enough in the flickering firelight. They were passing

around a bottle, lubricating their courage.
  He shook his head and smiled.
  Jake, Jake, Jake . . . you're a damned fool.

CHAPTER 19

Even if he'd had his Colt, four to one were long odds that Pike wouldn't have cared to buck.

There had to be another way.

Milner sat with his back to the oaks, behind him a thick tangle of underbrush. Pike considered that. Could he still sneak well enough to get behind Jake and use his knife?

He had no other options. It had to be done.

In drink, men talk loud and Milner and his boys were no exception. Talking even louder than the others, Jake was regaling them about Loretta's attributes and promising sexual joys to come for everybody.

"How hard can we ride her, Mr. Milner?" a man asked, laughing.

"Why, until she's broke," Milner said.

"Hell, I'm gonna enjoy that," the man said.

"An' I'm gonna enjoy watching you," Milner said.

More laughter. The bottle made its rounds.

Pike was on his feet, crouched, walking through the darkness, thinking carefully about every step he took.

Circling wide, he finally made the cover of the oaks. His eyes glittered with reflected firelight as he calculated the distance still remaining between him and Milner.

It seemed like a long way and dangerous.

Then Pike got a break.

A wise man once said that luck is what happens when preparation meets opportunity. Pike had prepared himself and now his opportunity arose.

Milner stood and said: "Boys, I'm gonna take a piss."

To Pike's joy, the man walked into the oaks and stopped just a few feet from where he lay crouched and hidden.

Milner grunted as his piss hissed on the grass. Pike worked his way behind him. He covered the last of the distance in two strides and placed the edge of the knife blade against the man's throat.

"Move a muscle, Jake, and I'll butcher you like a hog," Pike said.

Milner did not move, but he squealed in

terror, a raw shriek that brought his hired hands to their feet.

Pushing Milner ahead of him, Pike stepped closer to the fire.

As hands went to holstered guns, Pike said: "Tell them, Jake."

"Don't draw down on him, for God's sake," Milner screamed. "He'll kill me for sure."

"It's over for you boys," Pike said. "Get on your horses and head on home."

The three men were city toughs wearing corduroy pants, lace-up boots and plug hats. They didn't look like gunfighters, but Pike was well aware that they'd be a handful in a fight.

Right then, they didn't look pleased.

"Tell them again, Jake," Pike said. The knife pressed deeper into the big pimp's throat.

"You heard him," Milner said. His voice broke like a boy's. "It's over."

One of the toughs, a towhead with a broken nose, shook his head. "It ain't over until you pay us, Milner."

"I said I'd pay you when you killed a man," Milner said. He yelped as the blade sank deeper and drew a bead of blood. "Well, you ain't killed him on account he's got a knife at my throat."

Pike whispered into Milner's ear: "Get out your wallet, Jake. Real slow and easy. You and your boys scared the shit out of me and when I get scared I get violent and bad things happen."

The knife blade edged deeper.

"It's in my coat pocket, inside pocket," Milner said. His knees were trembling and piss ran down his leg.

"Get it, Jake," Pike said. "And give it to me."

Milner did as he was told. Pike tossed the wallet to the towhead.

"Wait, there's a hundred dollars in there," Milner wailed.

"You boys consider the extry a bonus," Pike said. "Now get out of here."

"Hey," the towhead said, "we was promised the woman."

"Too bad," Pike said. "Times are tough all over."

Another man said: "Hell, cowboy, at least give us a taste."

The sound of a racking Winchester was loud in the silence. "The only taste you boys are gonna get is a taste of lead," Loretta said.

She stood partially in shadow, the rifle butt resting on a cocked hip.

The three toughs considered their options

and didn't like any of them.

"Hell, I never did cotton to an uppity whore anyhow," the towhead said.

Loretta moved beside Pike, reached into the pocket of her dress and passed him his Colt.

"How you doing, Jacob?" she said.

"You stay away from my balls, bitch," Milner said.

"Still smarting, huh?" Loretta said.

Pike took his blade from Milner's throat. He pushed the man in front of him and jammed the muzzle of his Colt against the back of Milner's head.

"Make a fancy move and I'll scatter your brains, Jake," he said.

The three toughs decided they were bucking a stacked deck and threw in their hands. They made their way to their horses, but the towhead stopped and stared at Pike.

"You're from Texas, right?"

"Yup, you got it," Pike said.

"Are all you rannies as fast with the iron as they claim?"

"Who claims?"

"Folks around."

"Some of us are, some of us ain't," Pike said.

"How about you?" the towhead said.

"I'm among them as are," Pike said.

"No offense," the towhead said. "Just askin'."

"Well, now you know," Pike said.

He watched the toughs ride away, then smiled as Milner said: "What about me?"

"What about you, Jake?"

"Are you planning to let me go?"

"I'm taking you with us, Jake, all the way to Texas," Pike said. "You're what you might call my insurance policy."

"Those tramps won't come back," Milner said. "Not when they got half my supplies and all my money to spend on whiskey and whores in Santa Fe."

"There's truth in what you say, Jake," Pike said. "But I reckon I'll take you along just in case." He said to Loretta, "Pick up Jake's gun belt and rifle from beside the fire. We wouldn't want to be giving him ideas."

"You just keep that whore away from my balls," Milner said.

Pike said: "I know how you feel, Jake. She can be a trial and a tribulation at times."

"And damned mean enough to pitch her bathwater on a widder woman's kindling," Milner said, his face tight. "I wish I'd never set eyes on her."

Milner had done himself well.

In his supply sack Pike found a slab of

137

bacon, coffee, a loaf of sourdough bread that had only a few spots of green on the crust and another bottle of whiskey.

The hour was late, but hungry as he was, Pike slowly filled the coffeepot at a trickling stream running off the Pecos while Loretta fried bacon and bread.

Milner was trussed up in rope, though Pike assured him it would only be a night-time inconvenience.

"You think you're pretty damned smart, cowboy, don't you?" Milner said.

Pike spoke around a mouthful of bread and bacon. "Not too smart, Jake, but a lot smarter than you," he said. "Course, that ain't saying much, you understand."

"You're an idiot, Jake," Loretta said, sounding only half interested.

Milner opened his mouth to speak, but Pike said: "I'd think twice before you sass her, Jake. Remember what happened the last time."

The man let it go, but stared hard at Pike. "Things are gonna change oncet we get to Texas."

"How do you reckon on that?"

"I got friends there. You ever hear tell of Clem Dredge? Him and John Martin Simpson?"

Pike was surprised, but he didn't let it

show. "Can't say as I have, Jake."

"You will, cowboy," Milner said. "Me and Clem are like kinfolk. You was talking to the towhead about you being a Texas shootist an' all, but the Texan ain't been born that's a patch on Clem Dredge with the iron. An' Simpson ain't no slouch either."

"How come you keep such low company, Milner?" Loretta said.

"I done favors for Clem in the past," Milner said. "Gave him a place to hole up when the law was crowding him, loaned him a grubstake when he needed it. As I said, we're like kin."

Pike smiled. "Texas is a big state, Jake."

"Don't you go taking comfort in that, cowboy," Milner said. "Clem Dredge will cut Texas down to size."

CHAPTER 20

Following the old Butterfield Stage route, Pike and Loretta, with Milner in tow, crossed into Texas south of the Staked Plains.

"The Pecos is to the west of us," Pike told Loretta. "My ranch is about a five-day ride to the southeast." He looked at Milner. "I'm still a fur piece off my home range, but I'm cutting you loose, Jake."

Around them stretched rolling grass and brush plains, broken up by outcroppings of limestone rock and stands of oak, hickory and cedar.

It was not yet noon, but the day was already hot. To the south, clouds were gathering over the sky islands of the Davis Mountains, misting their pine-covered slopes that rose out of the surrounding Chihuahuan Desert.

"You haven't seen the last of me, Pike," Milner said.

Pike sighed. "Jake, you're a low-down, yellow dog and nothing you say scares me." He pointed back toward the Staked Plains. "The way to Santa Fe lies in that direction."

"I need my guns back," Milner said. "And I don't even have a dollar to buy a drink. The whore took my roll and you gave away the rest."

Pike turned in the saddle. "Loretta, give him his guns."

"You sure, Charlie?" Loretta said.

"I'm sure. He won't use them, at least not now."

Milner hung his gun belt on the saddle horn and slid his rifle in the boot. "I got no money," he said.

Pike waited to see if Loretta would volunteer. She didn't. Pike spun a dollar to Milner. "That will buy you a drink, Jake," he said.

"One day I'll kill you, Pike," Milner said, his eyes ugly. "And the whore. Depend on it."

He swung his horse away and rode north.

Pike watched him go, then said: "Loretta, you're welcome to stay at my ranch until you get settled."

"Best offer I've had today, Charlie," Loretta said.

She looked around her, at the empty vast-

141

ness of the land.

"I thought for sure Henry would have come back to us by now," she said.

"Do you miss him?" Pike asked.

"Hell no, I don't miss him. I just wonder where he is."

"Heading for Waco," Pike said. "That would be my guess."

"Then we're well rid of him."

Pike shook his head. "I don't think we're rid of him. He'll be back."

Loretta picked at a loose thread on her frayed and stained dress. "I'm in rags, Charlie," she said. "Look at this dress."

"Seems fine to me," Pike said.

"It ain't fine, Charlie. I need some clothes and other stuff. Isn't there a town around here?"

"There's a fair-sized settlement called Pecos twenty-five miles south of here," Pike said. "The Goodnight and Chisholm trails pass through the place and it's on a stage route. I reckon you'll find what you need there."

"You don't mind?" Loretta said. "I can head there myself and catch up with you later."

"It's on my way home," Pike said. "Besides, I need the makings. I ran out two days ago and it's been a trial to me since."

"So that's why you've been meaner than a sore-assed bear," Loretta said.

"Yeah, that and the fact that Jake was starting to wear on me."

"Charlie, you take care. He meant what he said about trying to kill you."

Pike nodded. "I plan to take care. There's nothing on God's earth more dangerous than a coward with a gun."

Pecos was a Western town like many others, but it wore its prosperity on its sleeve without a blush.

A dozen saloons were doing a roaring business when Pike and Loretta rode in and cow ponies lined the hitching rails.

Although darkness had fallen, three banks were still open for business, as were the general stores and the town blacksmith still pounded at his anvil.

Lamps were lit in the windows of the houses of the residential area. All the homes were set behind the town's business district, most with fenced, tidy yards that grew fine crops of prickly pear.

To Loretta's joy, a store advertising itself as THE NEW YORK HAT AND DRESS SHOP was ablaze with light. A couple of the local belles, fashionably attired in dresses with huge bustles, tiny hats perched on their upswept curls, walked out of the door carrying flat, white boxes, tied with pink ribbon.

"I'm going in there, Charlie," Loretta said, her eyes alight.

Pike glanced along the street. His gaze rested on the Alamo Saloon and Dance Hall, kitty-corner from where he sat his horse.

"When you come out, I'll be over there at the Alamo," Pike said.

"You don't want to come in, Charlie?" Loretta asked. She smiled, showing she didn't really mean it.

But Pike, in no mood to be teased, took her seriously. "I don't know anything about women's fixin's," he said.

"Pity. I always appreciate a man's opinion when I'm choosing bloomers."

"I'll be in the saloon," Pike said.

He found a place for his horse at the hitching rail and stepped inside.

The crowd was what Pike expected in any Texas boomtown. Punchers in big hats and high-heeled boots, spurs the size of teacups that chimed with every step, rubbed shoulders with a scattering of bearded miners, businessmen in broadcloth, hard-eyed ten-cents-a-dance girls, harder-eyed whores, pale gamblers, loungers, bummers and a few careful men with the watchful look of outlaws on the dodge.

One man stood out from the rest.

He had his back to the boisterous crowd, but his eyes never left the mirror behind the bar, apparently unconcerned, but seeing everything. He lifted his whiskey glass only with his left hand, his right hanging close to his gun.

Pike knew the type.

The man was a gun-for-hire. He looked prosperous and was therefore probably good at his job.

In the past, Pike had hired a couple of such men as extra hands at roundup. For whatever reasons, they'd been reduced to riding the grub line, but, as he recalled, they'd done their work without complaint and had given him no trouble.

Pike ordered a whiskey and a beer and tobacco and papers from the glass case on the bar.

The bartender served him, scooped up the dollar Pike had left on the bar and whispered, his eyes averted: "Buff Kelly at the bar. Just be real sociable."

"He'll get no trouble from me," Pike said.

And the bartended smiled and nodded.

Pike ordered another whiskey, then talked briefly to one of the local businessmen about cattle prices, the weather and the rancher W. S. Ikard's recent purchase of a Hereford bull from old Queen Vic's personal herd.

"Mark my words, cowboy," the man said, "in ten years the longhorn will be a thing of the past. Them white-faced cattle will take over the whole Texas range."

"It's never going to happen," Pike said. "Tick fever and winter graze will kill that bull quicker'n scat. The longhorn was made for Texas, or Texas was made for the longhorn, I don't rightly know which."

The businessman seemed unconvinced and was talking about how even Charlie Goodnight was buying Herefords, but Pike was only half listening.

A small, wizened man had stepped beside the gunfighter called Buff Kelly. The new arrival had no waist gun, but he carried a sawn-off Greener. He looked as brown and tough as old saddle leather and he would be a hard man to kill.

The businessman had asked Pike a question.

"Huh?" Pike said, blinking.

The man shook his head, irritated. "I'll leave you to your thoughts," he said, then turned and walked away.

Kelly and the small man were talking, loud enough for Pike to hear.

"You're not easy to find, McCone," Kelly said.

"I get around," McCone said. "Finally got your telegram at Fort Concho."

"I sent it there because I heard you were scouting for the Tenth Cavalry," Kelly said.

"You heard right."

"You're here," Kelly said. "I guess that means you're taking me up on my job offer."

"Five dollars a day, fifty-dollar bonus when the job's done. Those still the terms?"

"Yeah."

"Then I'm taking you up on your job offer."

"Drink?" Kelly asked.

"Coffee."

After the bartender had placed a steaming cup in front of McCone, Kelly said: "You're lucky, McCone. I planned on pulling out tomorrow."

"Man makes his own luck."

After waiting until McCone tried his coffee, Kelly said: "You stepped right up to me. How did you know I was the one sent the telegram?"

The small man allowed himself the ghost of a smile. "I was in Fort Worth when you kilt Blackie Jackson at the livery."

Kelly was stung. "I'll tell you what I tell

147

everybody else — he gave me back talk."

"So I heard."

"I can't abide an uppity nigger."

"As you say."

"Damn him, he had a pitchfork."

"I guess ol' Blackie hadn't studied up on the rule that says a man with a pitchfork doesn't go up against a man with a scatter-gun," McCone said.

"Damn right he hadn't," Kelly said.

Pike drank beer and wiped foam off his mustache with the back of his hand. He avoided making eye contact with Kelly.

"I only track, Kelly," McCone said. "If there's killing to be done, I leave that to men like you."

"You find the ranny the boss is looking for and you'll have done your job," Kelly said.

"Just wanted you to know," McCone said. He waited long enough to drain his coffee cup, then said: "Who is the boss?"

"You'll find out."

"Where's the job, or is that also a secret?"

"We start in Waco and go from there."

"Am I tracking a man who walks a wide path?"

Kelly smiled. "None wider."

"Then when do I start?"

"We'll pull out for Waco at first light tomorrow."

"Why not now, make some time?"

"Because I want more whiskey and a woman," Kelly said. "And I'm not even sure the boss is in Waco yet."

"Hell, Kelly, you're a man of mystery," McCone said.

"And you're starting to bore me," Kelly said. "Meet me at the livery stable at sunup. Now get the hell out of here."

"I can tell it's going to be a pleasure doing business with you," McCone said.

After the little man left, Pike felt Kelly's cold stare on him. He busied himself building a cigarette.

After what seemed an eternity, out of the corner of his eye, Pike saw Kelly mentally shrug and look away.

"Bartender, another whiskey," Kelly said.

And Pike quietly released his pent-up breath.

CHAPTER 21

Loretta did another little pirouette. "Well, what do you think, Charlie?"

"You look real good, Loretta," Pike said.

"I should. You know how much all this stuff cost me?"

"I don't, but I can imagine."

"The dresses are the very latest, all the way from Paris, France," Loretta said. "And the underwear."

"Class shows," Pike said. "You don't look like —" He bit his tongue.

"A whore?"

"I didn't mean —"

"I am a whore, Charlie," Loretta said. "I'm not ashamed to look like one. It's an ancient and honorable profession."

She smiled. "What will your little school-teacher think?"

"I reckon she's seen a whore before."

"Maybe I'll break her heart, Charlie."

"How come?"

150

"She'll reckon you're doing me."

"Maxine doesn't think that way."

"Oh no? But you've already done her. How else would she think?"

"Maxine is a respectable woman, Loretta."

"She's unmarried and knocked up, Charlie. How respectable can she be?"

Pike felt a flare of irritation. "What are you driving at, Loretta?"

"Nothing. I just want to make her jealous."

"Well . . ." Pike began. "Well, hell. I'm not going to discuss Maxine with you, Loretta."

"Suit yourself, Charlie."

"Damn it, Loretta," Pike said. "She won't be jealous."

"I'll be living at your ranch, Charlie. The bitch will want to scratch my eyes out."

Loretta picked up her new clothes from the bed and put them over her arm. "Now get back to your own room. The desk clerk is sending me up a bathtub."

Pike rose to his feet, the chair scraping behind him.

"Something you should know," he said.

Loretta paused. "Tell me."

"I saw a man by the name of Kelly hire a tracker at the Alamo tonight. I think Kelly is working for Clem Dredge and the man he wants found is Henry Dryden."

"And I should be concerned, why?" Loretta said.

"I still owe him, Loretta. I told him I'd get him to Texas so he could die peaceful. I can't turn my back on him now."

"He quit on us, remember," Loretta said. "You don't owe him a damned thing."

"I've been trying to tell myself that. But if I turn him away now, I'll be doing a great wrong."

"Then what's the right thing to do, Charlie?"

"I have to save him from Dredge. Then I've paid a debt I've owed since the Wilderness and it's done, over."

"How are you planning to save him, Charlie?"

"I've studied on that. I can't chase all over Texas after him, but the judge knows where my ranch lies, or he can find out easily enough. He'll come to me, Loretta, I know he will. And when he does, I'll do my best to protect him."

"You do what you think you have to, Charlie," Loretta said. "But count me out. I think Dryden is using you, like he's used so many other people in his life, including me."

"Loretta, I'm still beholden to him for my life. If I let that go, I can never again hold up my head in the company of men."

"Henry will take you to hell with him, Charlie."

"Then Clem Dredge will go with us. Depend on it."

Pike's ranch lay close to the Pecos, a few miles north of the Mexican border. It had good grass, a ready supply of water and was protected from the worst of hard winter weather by the Stockton Plateau to the north and the Sierra Madres to the south.

Loretta was less than impressed.

"This is where you live, Charlie?" she said.

"Home, sweet home," Pike said.

Pike meant what he said. But Loretta saw his modest place with different eyes and had her own opinion.

The ranch house was a low, squat cabin with a slightly swaybacked roof. A pole corral butted against the east side of the house and beyond lay a barn and blacksmith shop. The bunkhouse was no larger than a shack, enough to sleep four men, with a grudging stream running nearby. A smokehouse, a two-holer outhouse, a chicken coop and a few storage sheds made up the rest of the buildings.

Shabby as it was, the ranch was not run-down and was about as good as it got for a small rancher in 1880 west Texas.

Billy Childes greeted them from the bunkhouse door.

"Welcome back, boss," he said. "You're just in time for breakfast."

"We could use it," Pike said.

One of the hands Pike had hired for the roundup was snorting as he washed his face at a basin. The other was using a roller towel that had seen better days.

"Where's Sanchez?" Pike said.

"He pulled out three days ago. His pa is sick down to Piedras Negras way an' he says he don't know when he'll be back."

Pike felt a pang of concern. Sanchez was fast with the iron and a good man to have around.

Childes was looking at him expectantly.

"Oh, this is Miss Loretta Lamont," Pike said. "She'll be staying with us for a spell. Loretta, my foreman and *segundo*, Billy Childes."

Childes touched his hat. "Pleased to make your acquaintance, ma'am."

He looked puzzled, then shocked, when Loretta said: "Where's that bitch Maxine, Billy?"

CHAPTER 22

Billy Childes' jaw dropped. "Ma'am?"

"Where is she? Inside, waiting for poor Charlie with a loaded shotgun?"

Pike said: "Loretta, sitting horses in my front yard isn't the time or the place —"

"Don't you want to know, Charlie?"

Hunched miserably in the saddle, Pike said: "Yeah, I guess I do."

"Hell, she's hitched, boss," Childes said.

It was Pike's turn to be shocked. "To who?"

"To whom," Loretta said.

"Know that feller, name's Jamison, manages the general store for old Isaac Hurley over to town?" Childes said.

"Him with the bad leg an' turned eye?" Pike said.

"That's him. Well, he up an' got hitched to Maxine. It was kinda suddenlike. Seems he knocked her up over a barrel of soda crackers at the back of the store."

Loretta grinned. "And here, all the time you thought you were the daddy, Charlie."

She looked at Childes. "Is she showing?"

"Not so you'd notice, ma'am. She's still teaching at the schoolhouse."

"Hey, Charlie, seems like Maxine wanted a husband real bad," Loretta said. "You had a narrow escape, huh?"

Pike was thinking. Then he said: "Over a barrel of soda crackers. How the hell did he manage that?"

"I'll tell you one day, Charlie," Loretta said. She looked at Childes. "Hey, Billy, don't buy any soda crackers from the general store for a while, huh?"

As was his habit, Pike ate with the hands, Childes and a couple of taciturn older men from the Nueces River country.

After breakfast was over, cigarettes were lit and Childes said: "I've been keeping the real good news for last, boss."

"I could use some," Pike said.

"Cavalry sergeant passed by the other day, says Fort Stockton will buy all the Indian beef we can drive that way," Childes said. "With ol' Nana an' Geronimo an' them playing hob, the army wants to keep its tame Apaches fed."

"What are they paying?"

156

"Top dollar, boss."

"How much?"

"Ten dollars for yearlings, fifteen for two-year-olds," Childes said. "I reckon we can drive seventy head of mixed stuff and clear a profit of six hundred, easy."

Getting no response, Childes stared at Pike. "We need the money, Charlie."

"I know that, Billy, but I can't make the drive with you," Pike said. "I got business here."

Pike saw the old-fashioned look Childes cast at Loretta and said quickly: "Judge Dryden will be coming this way. I want to be around when he gets here."

"Hangin' Hank is coming here?" Childes said.

Pike nodded. "He's on the run, Billy."

"Who's chasing him?"

"Man by the name of Clem Dredge and a gunfighter who calls himself John M. Simpson."

Childes whistled through his teeth. "He sure don't pick his enemies very well. Just one of them two is a handful. Together they'll raise more hell than a couple of alligators in a drained swamp."

"The judge knows that."

"Did you get Hank to Texas?"

Pike hesitated, then said: "Yeah, he's in Texas."

"Then you don't owe him nothing, boss. You can't handle Dredge and J. M. Simpson."

"Throw in a man called Buff Kelly while you're at it," Pike said.

"Him as shot Blackie Jackson down Fort Worth way for sassin' him?"

"The very same."

Childes shook his head. "Then we ain't driving no herd to the army, not this spring." He looked at the two drovers. "What do you say, boys?"

The older of the two, a lantern-jawed man with store-bought teeth, drank coffee before he answered. "Billy, we signed on for the roundup and we'll drive your herd to Fort Stockton, but we're not bucking draw fighters. Not Clem Dredge and John Simpson, we ain't."

Childes looked at the younger of the two, a man named Jones. "Is Parkman talking for you, Jed?"

"He said it, Billy."

"You're a pair of sorry, no-good —"

"It don't matter, Billy," Pike said quickly. "We need the six hundred dollars. The barn roof has dry rot and needs sawn lumber, the corral is falling down and we want to put in a well."

He looked at Childes. "You, Jed and Tom Parkman can drive the herd."

"And leave you here by yourself, boss?" Childes said.

"I can handle it."

Childes' eyes were pleading. "Boss, you don't owe that damned hanging judge nothing."

Pike was irritated and his voice rose to a shout. "I owe him. Now let it go, Billy."

Seeing the hurt expression on the foreman's face, Pike softened. "Just . . . gather the herd and get that army money. As always, I'm depending on you, Billy."

Loretta, who had been silent until now, sat back in her chair. "Well, this has been pleasant. Just what I needed to settle burned salt pork and raw beans."

Childes and the two drovers left with the herd at first light the next morning.

Pike shook hands with all three and Childes smiled, letting him know that nothing bad lay between them.

"Be back in two weeks, boss," he said. "Maybe less."

"Take care, Billy."

"You too, boss. Take care."

■ ■ ■ ■

Loretta was sitting in Pike's favorite chair when he returned to the cabin. He had a small library of books and Loretta was reading Sir Walter Scott's *The Fair Maid of Perth.*

"Good book?" Pike said.

"I don't know, Charlie, I've only started it."

Loretta made an inverted V of the book on her lap. "Where do we go from here, Charlie?"

"We wait."

"I won't wait for long," Loretta said. "I have to be going soon."

"Where?"

"I don't know. San Antone maybe."

"Will you go back to the whoring trade?"

"I reckon so. It's all I've known since I was thirteen. I'm comfortable with it."

A silence stretched, then Loretta said: "How come you've never tried to screw me, Charlie?"

"I wouldn't be comfortable with it."

"Because I'm a whore?"

"No, I reckon not. It's just that it don't seem right."

"I don't seem right?"

"For me? No, it don't."

"You never need make a commitment to a whore, Charlie. Didn't your mama ever tell you that?"

"No, she never did."

Loretta sighed and picked up her book. "Ah well, it's your loss, Charlie."

Pike smiled. "Would you charge me?"

"Of course. I'm a whore, remember?"

A small silence, then Loretta said, looking up from her book: "Did you love her, Charlie?"

"Who?"

"Maxine. Who else?"

"I guess. Maybe. I don't rightly know."

"Do you love her now?"

"No. Well, thinking on it, I still do, a little."

"You're a good man, Charlie, but you're not too clever. How did you ever get to be a major?"

Pike smiled. "Everybody else got killed. I guess they had to promote somebody. As for not being clever, I'd say you're right. At any rate, I was stupid enough to walk into a round of Yankee canister."

Loretta dropped her eyes to her book again. "Charlie, you don't know much about anything, including women and, worst of all, you don't know that loyalty has its limits."

Looking back on it, Pike could never

remember what he was going to say next, since the bullet that splintered through the cabin door effectively ended all conversation.

Chapter 23

"You in the cabin! Get out here! We want to talk to you."

Pike took a rifle from the rack, levered a round into the chamber and opened the door a crack. "What do you want?"

"Jus' talk, señor. No more bang-bang."

This from a Mexican who sat a wiry, mouse-colored mustang. Beside him the young, blond man with the handlebar mustache seemed impatient and irritated.

"Come out here, Pike," this man said. "We're not gonna hurt you."

Pike thought things through. Neither rider seemed ready for a gunfight, their rifles booted under their knees, holstered Colts riding high on their waists.

Loretta had stepped to the window.

"I don't like the look of this, Charlie," she said.

"Me neither," Pike said. "But I don't want them turning my cabin into a sieve."

He opened the door wide and stepped into the yard.

The Mexican's face was shadowed by the wide brim of his sombrero, but his black eyes were glittering.

"Ah, where is my fren' Pedro Ramirez Heladio Sanchez?" he asked.

Pike thought about lying, saying Sanchez was close by, but the Mexican would see through that.

"His pa is sick, down Piedras Negras way," Pike said. "He's gone to be with him."

The Mexican crossed himself. "May God speed his recovery." He smiled, showing a mouthful of gold teeth. "I am disappointed, señor. Pedro and me have a thing to settle. You understand?"

Then Pike remembered. "You must be Mexican Bob. I've heard Pete talk about you."

The man's golden smile grew wider. "There are many men who call themselves Mexican Bob, señor."

"Yeah, but if you're the one Pete was talking about, none of them are a patch on you."

"All right, enough of this," the towhead said. "Pike, I'm gonna ask you a question. Answer it truthfully and we'll all part friends."

"Ask away, Kelly," Pike said.

"I guess Sanchez mentioned my name too, huh?"

"Nah, my foreman did. Said you're the man who killed Blackie Jackson."

Kelly was irritated and it showed in the way his mouth tightened under his mustache. "I've killed nine white men, but all anybody remembers is that damned nigger."

"Ask your question," Pike said, pleased that Kelly had been stung.

"Where is Henry Dryden?"

"I don't know."

"Has he been here?"

"No."

"Are you lying to me, Pike?"

"Don't call me a liar, Kelly."

The muzzle of Pike's rifle rose an inch and Kelly read the sign.

"When did you last see Dryden?" he asked, tiptoeing away from a direct confrontation.

Kelly wasn't scared, Pike could see that, but the man wanted information, not a close-up gunfight.

At least, not now.

"I last saw him two weeks ago," Pike said. "Maybe a day or two less."

"Where was he headed?"

"I don't know. Texas, I guess."

Pike took a step toward Kelly. The man's

big American stud tossed its head in annoyance, the bit ringing.

"Why does Clem Dredge want Judge Dryden?" Pike said.

He knew the answer. He just wanted to hear Kelly say it.

"Clem means to kill him for hanging his brother."

"Where is Dredge?"

"Close."

The Mexican spoke again. "Señor Dredge is just across the border only ten miles due south of where we stand," he said. "The village is called San Fermin and you can find it easily."

He sat back in the saddle. "If you hear of this hombre Dryden, you will come tell Señor Dredge. It will be better for you if you do it quickly, I think."

"Pike, you heard the man," Kelly said.

"And if I ignore him?"

"Then you'll hang alongside Dryden."

Pike spent the next few days doing odd jobs around the ranch, but his restlessness grew as did his irritation with Loretta.

She kept her nose buried in *The Fair Maid of Perth,* engrossed in the beautiful Catherine Glover's love for Henry Smith the armorer. She showed little interest in Simpson's threats or the whereabouts of Dryden.

Finally Pike couldn't take the waiting any longer.

"I'm going to poke around, see what I can see," he said one night after supper. "I'll be gone for a couple of days. Will you be all right by yourself?"

Loretta smiled at him. "Charlie, I've been taking care of myself since I was fourteen. I think I can manage for a few days without your help."

"Keep a loaded rifle by the door and don't trust anybody," Pike said.

"I'll try to remember that."

"And if Dryden shows up, tell him to stay put and wait."

"I may shoot him with my loaded rifle."

Pike gave Loretta a hard stare.

"Just joking, Charlie. I'll invite him inside and we'll have tea."

"He's a hunted man. He won't hurt you."

"Damn right he won't. I'll never let him use a dog whip on me again."

"He did that?"

"You don't want to know, Charlie."

"Sometimes I wonder —"

"If Henry Dryden's life is worth saving?"

"A traitorous thought, I guess."

"No, it's not. Judge Henry Dryden is a piece of shit. I know it and now you're beginning to know it."

Pike made no answer and Loretta said: "Struck dumb, Charlie?"

"I reckon I'll take the buckskin tomorrow, let the sorrel rest up longer," he said.

"Sometimes no answer is the most honest answer of all," Loretta said.

CHAPTER 24

Pike crossed the Rio Bravo and into Mexico with one destination in mind — the village of San Fermin where Dredge was holed up. He had no firm course of action in mind, but if he got a clear shot at the outlaw . . .

That would end everyone's problems and he'd finally be off the hook as far as Dryden was concerned.

But he wasn't a bushwhacker. He couldn't backshoot a man in cold blood. Neither could he face Dredge in a gunfight. Or Simpson or the Mexican or Kelly or probably any of them.

His options limited, Pike rode on aimlessly . . . like a man lost in a misty dreamscape.

He camped for the night in a grove of mixed oak and pine among the rolling foothills of the High Sierras.

Pike took to the trail again at sunup and by noon saw the village in the distance, strung out along the near bank of a creek swollen by the last of the spring melt.

He swung out of the saddle and led the buckskin into the pines. He got a glass from his saddlebags and walked to a rise about twenty yards ahead of him.

Lying on his belly, the telescope to his eye, he studied the village.

Or what was left of it.

Several of the adobe buildings had been fired and the roof of one still smoldered, sending a trail of smoke into the air as straight as a plumb line.

There was a small plaza and what looked like a cantina. As he watched, a white man lurched out of the door, stood facing the wall and took a piss. He stumbled back inside again, buttoning up.

Moments later a drama unfolded that made Pike catch his breath and revealed the stamp of men he was dealing with.

A Mexican girl ran out the cantina, the white blouse torn from her shoulders so that her breasts were exposed. A big, bearded white man was right behind her. He grabbed the girl, slapped her viciously backhanded across the face and she dropped to the ground.

Angrily, a small Mexican man ran at the huge gringo, his fists flailing. The white man grinned, held his attacker at arm's length with his left, drew with his right.

He fired twice into the Mexican's body and the dark little man fell.

The American holstered his gun. He bent, grabbed the girl by an ankle and dragged her toward the cantina. Her skirt rode up, displaying the dark V of her complete nakedness.

A couple of men, Pike recognized one of them as Kelly, appeared in the cantina door, grinning, cheering on the bearded man. He dragged the girl inside and then the other two followed.

Pike snapped the telescope shut.

Had the big man been Clem Dredge?

That was likely, a fine, upstanding citizen and a credit to his race.

Pike was on a slow burn. He'd seen his mother abused and terrorized by a drunken brute of a husband and he could not bear to see any woman mistreated. Or child either.

His qualms about playing the bushwhacker forgotten, he walked back to the buckskin, got his rifle and returned to the rise.

When it came to wild animals like Clem Dredge, the game had no rules.

From where he lay to the door of the cantina was about a hundred yards. No great range for a competent rifleman, but Pike wasn't one of those.

He put the Winchester to his shoulder.

The sun was at its highest point, scorching the sky, raising white blisters of cloud. The Madres stretched away from him forever, timbered, dark green peaks that slowly faded to purple in the distance.

Flies droned around Pike's head and crickets played fiddle in the long grass.

His finger tightened on the trigger.

There were village women in the cantina and probably a few of their menfolk. Not uncaring, but coldly realistic, Pike reckoned the women would all be on their backs on the floor. The men would have to take their chances.

He sighted on the door and fired.

Nothing.

Pike had punched a hole in the timber door, he was sure, but it remained closed and there was no outcry from inside that he could hear.

Sighting carefully, sweat stinging his eyes, he fired again.

This time the reaction was immediate.

Men boiled out of the door like hornets from a kicked nest, guns in hand.

Pike got up on one knee. He dusted shots

at Dredge's men and saw one go down.

He smiled. Good shooting, Charlie!

It took the outlaws a few moments to figure out what was happening.

In that time, Pike scored another hit, on Dredge or a man who looked like him.

Now the outlaws realized what was happening and where the shots were coming from. Bullets thudded into the rise and splintered the air around Pike's head.

Crouched men were coming in his direction, led by a raging Dredge, who was bleeding from a wound in his left shoulder.

Pike left the ridge at a run, swung into the saddle of the buckskin and rode due west, away from the direction of his ranch.

It was unlikely that Dredge knew who his assailant was — but he'd come looking. That much was certain.

Pike rode for five miles, constantly studying his back trail. He spotted the dust cloud behind him as he splashed into a creek and stopped to let the buckskin drink.

Dredge and his men were coming on fast, a passel of them riding fresh horses, as relentless as a hanging posse.

Panic rising in him, Pike kneed his horse out of the water. The buckskin took a few steps, then hobbled to a stop, favoring his left foreleg.

Looking at the washed-out sky, Pike vented his lungs, cussing loud enough to scorch the feathers off one of the circling buzzards.

This was all he needed. Killers on his trail behind him and a lamed-up horse under him.

CHAPTER 25

Charlie Pike stepped out of the leather and crouched beside the buckskin's leg. All the way to the knee, the cannon was swollen and hot to the touch.

The horse wasn't going anywhere, not with a rider on its back.

Pike stood and looked behind him. The dust was much nearer, closing on him fast.

Sweat staining the back of his shirt, he gathered up the reins and walked the buckskin in the direction of the foothills.

He saw little that offered shelter for man and horse.

Here the breaks were shallow, covered in thorn scrub, ocotillo and scattered, stunted juniper, unlike the lush vegetation and deep, shady arroyos farther south.

Pike led the horse along the edge of the low hills, his eyes desperately searching. More scrub, mean little rises.

Dredge and his men were now only a few

minutes away. He could hear the throbbing drum of their running horses in the distance.

Quickly, Pike grabbed his canteen, rifle and supplies sack from the buckskin. He stripped the horse of saddle and bridle and slapped the animal away from him.

A man, more enduring, could go where a horse could not.

He ran into the foothills, dodging cactus, thorns tugging at his legs. The arroyo he had chosen was narrow, its sides coming only to his shoulders, but he plunged deeper.

Then he had a thought that chilled him to the bone.

Was McCone, the mean little tracker, with Dredge?

If he was, Pike could consider himself a dead man.

The ground under his feet climbed gradually, limestone shingle on sandy mud that had not yet dried from the spring runoff. A rock, shaped like a massive flatiron, loomed ahead of him, blocking his way. A trickle of water ran from the top of the boulder, splashing into a tank at its base.

His breath tearing loose from his chest, his heart hammering, Pike stopped at the flatiron. He cupped water in his hands, drank, then splashed more on his burning face.

He stood stock-still, listening into the uneasy afternoon.

Insects made small echoes in the grass, water cascaded softly into the rock tank and somewhere close a bird trilled.

Of booted and spurred men, there was no sound.

Pike fought down the urge to go back the way he'd come and see what was happening. But he knew it would be a bad move. By this time Dredge would have found the horse and would know the man who had wounded him was close.

Even now, Dredge and his men might be with McCone . . . waiting and grinning.

Water had gouged a narrow trench on both sides of the flatiron rock. The furrow to Pike's left was impossibly steep and slick, but the one on the right rose more gradually. Clumps of bunchgrass growing around it would provide something to grab on to.

Slinging the canteen and food sack over his shoulder, Pike took the rifle in his left hand and began to climb.

Ten minutes later, covered in mud from head to toe after slipping and sliding, once all the way back to the bottom, Pike made the top of the rock.

Here, behind the peak of the flatiron, the ground was level for thirty yards, then rose only gradually to a bare stone ridge. Juniper, piñon and a few cedars clustered on the flat and the slope and the ground was covered in deer and bear sign.

Again Pike stood and listened. He heard nothing.

Leaving behind the canteen and sack, he climbed to the ridge and looked over.

The ground fell away in a sheer, rocky slope, ending at a grassy plain that stretched a fair distance to the north and south. Beyond the flat rose a series of mountains that spiked their lilac peaks into the sky.

Pike decided he'd spend the night close to the ridge, then head down into the plain at first light.

Without a horse he'd be slow to cover ground and be dangerously exposed. But if Dredge and his men were watching the foothills, he had no other choice.

Pike had taken three steps toward the flatiron rock when the bullet hit him.

CHAPTER 26

"Clem, I got the son of a bitch!"

Pike heard the man yell at the same time he hit the ground.

He rolled into the meager cover of the junipers. Low down, just above his gun belt, his side was on fire.

Bullets hit around him and one smashed into the stock of his rifle with a hollow *thunk!* The shattered Winchester spun from Pike's grasp and he drew his Colt.

A tall man wearing a plug hat and a long Confederate greatcoat was running toward him, firing a rifle from his shoulder. Pike fired, missed. At a range of ten yards he shot again.

The man shrieked and went down hard, raising dust.

Glancing around him, Pike tried to assess his situation through eyes that were dimming with pain.

He had been outflanked, hit from two

sides by men who were better with guns than he was. He calculated his life expectancy could be measured in minutes.

A yell from his right. "Hey, Kelly, did Silas put a bullet into him?"

Buff Kelly's voice came from somewhere to his left. "Yeah."

"Where is he?"

"Who?"

"The bastard who bushwhacked us, you idiot!"

"He's in the trees, Clem, holed up."

"Where's Silas?"

"Dead, as close as I can tell. Leastways, he ain't moving."

Dredge's voice again. "Silas never did have a lick o' sense, him an' that tetched brother of his."

A tense minute ticked past.

Pike put his hand to his side and it came up bloody. He'd been hit hard. He wiped his hand on the grass at his side. Maybe he was dying. He didn't know.

"Hey, Kelly!"

"Yeah, Clem?"

"Where is that bastard?"

"Near as I can tell, in the bunch of junipers just under the ridge. Silas is lying real close to there."

"Hey, you in the trees," Dredge yelled.

Pike said nothing.

"You come out now, y'heah?" Dredge said. "Take your medicine like a man."

A silence stretched, grew thin and broke.

"You come out now and we'll do some talking, you an' me," Dredge said. "Hell, I'll probably let you live, fix you up good an' send you on your way."

Pike pushed his Colt out in front of him, looking for a target. He saw only trees, rock and lengthening shadows.

"What do you say, partner?" Dredge said. "Ain't that a true-blue offer I just made?"

Pike made no answer.

He tilted his head and looked at the sky where the sun was sliding lower and the few white clouds were tinged with pink.

How long until dark? Another hour, maybe more.

Pike lowered his head. He'd probably be dead by then. The moon would come out, looking for him, but he wouldn't be there.

Despite the pain in his side, despite his clamoring fear, Pike smiled at his bleak thoughts. Funny how a bullet in the gut can change a man's outlook on things.

"Hey, Kelly?" Dredge yelled.

"Yeah?"

"Me, Simpson an' the Mexican are gonna lay down some fire. You an' the three with you flush that son of a bitch out o' them trees and we'll gun him."

The afternoon grew tight, close, smelling of blood.

"Clem, I don't think he's a pilgrim," Kelly said. "He kilt Silas, mind."

Dredge's voice was edged with anger. "Kelly, you turning yellow on me?"

"I'm just saying he ain't a pushover, Clem."

"Do as I say, Kelly, or I'll kill you my own self."

Pike quickly reloaded the empty chambers of his Colt, then rammed the revolver hard into the holster. He got his feet under him.

He had two choices: Stay here and be slaughtered by Dredge — or commit suicide.

If he took the suicide route, he'd maybe one chance in a hundred of surviving. If he stayed where he was, he had no chance at all.

Kelly and those with him had yet to make a move. But bullets were clipping through the trees around Pike as Dredge and his men opened fire.

It was now or never.

Pike swallowed hard, turned and made a run for the ridge.

He almost made it without a scratch. But just as he jumped, a bullet smashed into his left elbow with the force of a sledgehammer.

Then he was sailing through the air, the slope beyond the ridge rushing up fast to meet him. Pike hit feetfirst and began to tumble, cartwheeling down the rise, thudding against rocks in his passing.

As sky and land spun around him, he felt a tremendous blow to his head.

Then he knew no more.

CHAPTER 27

Pike woke to the flickering ghosts of lamp-light.

He stirred, wondering where he was. He was in a bed, a soft mattress under him, a blanket covering him to the shoulders.

Above him, a pine-log ceiling, the beams ruddy from reflected fire but dark in the corners where the spinning spiders lived.

A man's face swam into view. Bald head, broken nose, a gray beard spreading across his chest. His eye sockets were pooled with shadow.

"Where am I?" Pike said.

"In my cabin," the man said. "We're at a place the Mexicans call the Arroyo de la Zorra. I don't know what the Apaches call it."

"How far to the Rio Bravo?"

"Fifty miles. As the crow flies."

"My name is Charlie Pike. I have a ranch up on the Pecos."

184

"You can call me Zachary."

"Prospector?"

"Healer."

Pike managed a smile. "I fell in with the right company."

He tried to look into the eyes of the man named Zachary, but they were lost in darkness.

"Did you find me?" Pike said.

"No, some Mexicans did. They thought you were an evil mountain spirit, so they brought you to me."

"How long ago?"

"A week."

"I've been out of it for a week?"

"Longer. I'd say at least three weeks before the Mexicans brought you here."

Pike tried to think, his brain reeling. "But how —"

"Did you survive?"

"Yeah, how?"

"Mexicans from the villages around here say you were wandering among the trees for a long time, grubbing for roots, berries, whatever you could find. When they got too close, you fired your gun at them."

"I don't remember that."

"You took a blow to your head at some point. It made you a little crazy."

"A little crazy?" Pike said. "I must have

been completely out of my mind."

"I'd say that."

Zachary placed a hand on Pike's forehead. "Fever's down. Think you can eat?"

"I'm hungry."

The man left and Pike started to piece together what he could remember.

Dredge and his men . . . the wound in his side . . . killing the man named Silas . . . his suicide jump off the ridge . . . tumbling. . . . hitting the rocks . . .

Loretta. Judge Dryden. The ravaged Mexican village. Sunshine and Shadow. Darkness. The moon spiked on trees . . .

Memories, fragile as gossamer, cobwebbed his brain.

He tried to struggle to a sitting position. He shouldn't be here. He had to get back to his ranch.

"Easy, my friend, easy," Zachary said. He held a steaming bowl. "Beef broth. It will give you strength."

Pike reached out for the food. Only his right hand moved. He tried to lift his left arm. The blanket rose only a little.

"What the hell?" he said. "Am I paralyzed?"

Now he saw Zachary's eyes, bright, sky blue, concerned, sympathetic. But old.

"Charlie, I couldn't save your arm," he

said. "The elbow was smashed and it was rotten. Gangrene would have killed you."

The shock plunged Pike into a babbling wreck.

"Maggots. The maggots must have saved me. I remember in the Wilderness . . . maggots . . . thousands . . . thousands of maggots . . ."

"There were no maggots, Charlie. Only black rot. I'm sorry."

With his right hand, Pike threw the blanket aside. Where his arm had been, there was only a bloody, bandaged stump that ended above his elbow.

He stared at Zachary, wanting to scream.

"You son of a bitch, what did you do to me?" he yelled. "You bastard, you stole my arm."

Pike tried to get out of the bed, felt Zachary's firm hand push him back. Now he did scream, his mouth wide open, head thrown back.

Then a terrible darkness took him again.

He never heard Zachary say: "Slumber soundly, Charlie. Sleep is surely one of God's tender mercies."

Chapter 28

Sunlight filtered through the cabin windows like gold lace, turning the dancing dust motes into tiny silver moths. A rising breeze rattled the door and window frames and tossed pine needles against the panes.

Pike lay in bed, again wondering where he was.

Then he remembered and the loss of his arm hit him like a blow to the face.

He heard footsteps and Zachary stood beside his bed.

"I've put the broth on to heat, Charlie," he said.

"I don't want any of your damned broth," Pike said. "You damned butcher."

"It was the only way I could save your life," Zachary said.

"What the hell good is a one-armed man to anybody? Damn you, you should have let me die."

Zachary was silent for a few moments;

then he said: "We were both in the war, Charlie. We saw a lot of men lose limbs."

"They were them. They were not me."

"I recall that not many of them wallowed in self-pity, though. They went on living."

Anger flared in Pike. "How do I sit a horse and rope a steer with one arm? Tell me that." He shook his head. "No, don't tell me, I'll tell you — it can't be done."

"You'll find a way, if you're willing to search for it." Zachary smiled. "I'll bring the broth."

"Get the hell away from me," Pike said.

The man stayed where he was. "Charlie, when the war ended, I vowed I'd never take another human life. I decided to become a healer. I'd save life, not destroy it."

He laid a hand on Pike's chest.

"But sometimes a man must make his own choices. If you choose to die, then I'll bury you decent and say the holy words. If you choose to live, I will do my best to make you strong again."

Zachary stepped away from the bed. He looked back at Pike.

"Be assured, if death is your preference, it will not be long in coming."

Charlie Pike's sleep was a walk through a terrifying darkness, heavy with mist, streaked scarlet by fire and the flash of cannon, hellish with the screams of dying men. He fell and maggots crawled all over him, feasting on his flesh.

Brigadier General Dryden, plumed, resplendent in gray and gold, mounted on a great black charger, drew rein and glanced down at him. Pike reached out a bloody hand where maggots squirmed.

"Help me, General," he said.

Dryden was outlined by a sky the color of slate, stained red by flames. He turned in the saddle and said to someone behind him: "See if he can be helped. If not, put him out of his misery."

He waved a hand. "Ride on."

A round, Irish face, bright blue eyes, sergeant's stripes on a muddy arm.

"Jesus, Mary and Joseph and all the saints in heaven, how did you get in this state, Major?"

"Help me," Pike said.

"I'm taking you back to the regimental surgeons. And they'll say that it's a sorry mess you're in, to be sure."

"Sergeant, am I going to die?"

"I'm not going to let you die, Major, me darlin'. There's been enough o' that already."

The soldier rose to his feet. "I'll be bringing me horse and a canteen. Now, don't be going anywhere until I get back."

Pike woke, this time with the full realization that his arm was gone.

Zachary heard him stir and stood beside the bed.

Pike looked up at him. "In the Wilderness . . . it wasn't Dryden who saved me. It was an Irish sergeant whose name I don't even know."

"Did you ever see him again, Charlie?"

"No."

"Maybe he was an angel. Irish, you say?"

"He looked and sounded Irish."

"Ah well, Charlie, I have no doubt that there are Irish angels."

"It wasn't Dryden."

"As you say, it wasn't him."

"My arm gone . . . the dead men. I did it all for nothing. I owed Dryden nothing."

"This man Dryden, he told you he saved your life?"

"Yes. Then he called in the favor."

"He lied to you."

"Yeah. I thought I owed him."

"Now you owe it to yourself to get well, Charlie."

"I'm hurting," Pike said.

"A bullet went clean through your side. I

think that wound is now on the mend."

"My arm, all the way to my fingers. Hurts."

"The hurt in your fingers is a phantom pain. With time it will go away. I'll give you something to help."

"I'm hungry."

Zachary smiled. "The broth is now good and thick. I made it with beef and plenty of wild onions."

"I could sure use some."

"You have chosen life, Charlie."

"Yeah. I've decided that I've got things to do."

CHAPTER 29

Zachary wasn't being cruel when he rousted Pike out of bed.

He knew the best way for the young man to regain his strength was to walk every day and he insisted on it.

After two weeks Pike felt stronger and his appetite improved.

Zachary dressed the stump of his arm with his own concoctions and it began to heal well, though pain was always with him.

A small corral with a horse shed with a slanted timber-and-tar-paper roof stood behind the cabin.

A rangy zebra dun was standing in the shed but stepped over to greet Pike when he leaned on the fence.

Pike stroked the dun's velvety nose, liking the smell of him.

"He's a good horse," Zachary said. "He's got plenty of bottom."

"I like him," Pike said.

"I don't ride him much any longer," Zachary said. "The Mexicans bring me all I need and so do the Apaches when they're around."

"I need a horse," Pike said.

He let it hang there.

"I figured you would, Charlie."

"Will you sell him?"

Zachary was silent. Pike looked at him. Despite the gray beard, the man could be any age, old, young, it was hard to tell. But he had scars on him. Pike saw it in his eyes.

"I'll loan him to you, Charlie," Zachary said.

"I'll bring him back," Pike said.

"I know you will."

Pike glanced at the sky. "Zachary, I'm beholden to you, but I have to be moving on."

"You're beholden to God, Charlie, not me. I'm only his instrument."

"The stump still hurts and it's mighty raw."

"It will be both things for a while. I'll give you a salve to put on it."

"When can I ride?"

"Anytime you feel like it. You're a tough man, Charlie, and your wounds healed fast."

That night after supper, Pike cleaned and oiled his gun. For the next two hours he practiced strapping on his gun belt with one hand. He ended up tired and sweaty and cursing, but finally learned how to manage it.

His rifle was gone. But even with two hands, he'd never been much good with a long gun anyway. The loss did not trouble him unduly.

A week later at daybreak, sitting Zachary's saddle, astride his horse, Pike was ready to leave.

He held out his hand to Zachary. "I don't have the words," he said.

"No words needed, Charlie. Take good care of my horse and yourself."

"You saved my life."

Zachary winked. "Maybe I'm an angel, though in my case I'd be a Dutch angel."

"You're an angel all right. And a fine man."

"Ride easy, Charlie. Take care."

Pike gathered up the reins and nodded. "I'll bring the horse back."

He rode away, heading north into the new aborning day.

Behind him Zachary called: "Don't forget the salve. Twice a day, now. Remember that, Charlie."

Pike's empty sleeve was tucked into his belt, but the fingers of his left hand burned.

■ ■ ■ ■

Two days later he crossed the Rio Bravo and under a threatening sky, he swung north toward his ranch.

Lightning burst open the clouds and rain fell in sheets, driven by a hulking wind that bent the pines and tossed needles across the trail. It had just gone noon, but it was dark among the trees and the visibility of the way ahead was reduced to less than fifty yards.

Pike had no slicker and was soaked to the skin, rain cascading off the brim of his hat. He swung into the ticking pines and stepped out of the saddle.

He had placed what was left of his makings in the saddlebags Zachary had provided. Now he tried to build a cigarette with one hand.

After some failed attempts, he found a way, as a man with the tobacco hunger will.

Standing beside the horse, Pike smoked and watched the driving rain.

He'd be home soon and Billy Childes or one of the hands would have lit a fire in the ranch house and Loretta would have coffee on the bile. He could use both.

Lighting forked across the sky, thunder crashed and even here, among the shelter of the pines, the wind found a way to bully Pike, pummeling him, giving him no peace.

The prospect of getting back on the trail was not to Pike's liking, but the storm showed no sign of letting up and his ranch was close.

He let his cigarette butt fall, hissing into wet grass, and swung into the saddle.

Boisterous rain, wind and lightning greeted him like a long-lost friend. Then did its best to make his life miserable.

Pike crossed the Rio Bravo, the downpour hissing into the shallow river like an angry dragon.

Ahead of him stretched the limestone-capped mesas, rolling hills and broad grassy plains of the Stockton Plateau, gray and bleak behind a torrential downpour and scudding wind that tossed the canopies of the cypress, willow and sycamore along the deep stream divides.

Slowed by weather, Pike took two hours to reach his ranch . . .

Or what was left of it.

Chapter 30

The ranch house was burned to the ground, as was the barn and smokehouse. The pole corral had been ripped apart and the two-holer outhouse, a luxurious feature that was a source of great pride to Pike, was tipped over, smashed into splinters.

Only the bunkhouse was more or less intact, though the door had been ripped off and the iron stove chimney torn down.

Pike swung out of the saddle and walked to the ranch house.

His eyes saw, but could not yet comprehend, the destruction that had happened here.

A few blackened spars of wood stuck up from the ashes, but the stone fireplace still stood, like the ruin of an ancient temple.

Pike bent and picked up a scorched and waterlogged book from the ground. *The Fair Maid of Perth* had survived to continue her lively love affair.

Pike was still holding the book, his head bowed in the rain, when Billy Childes found him.

The *segundo* made two statements, close together, the second a question. "Boss, you're alive." And, "Where the hell is your arm?"

"Yeah, I'm alive, Billy. As for the arm, I left it in Mexico."

Childes was not a fast thinker and Pike saw him search his mind for the right words. He took that responsibility away from him.

"Who did this, Billy?" Pike said.

"I don't know, boss."

"When did it happen?"

"Three weeks ago, the day me and the hands got back from Fort Stockton."

"You were here when it happened?"

"No. We saw the smoke from a distance. When we got here, it was all over."

"Loretta?"

"I don't know."

"Maybe she escaped."

"I don't know, boss."

"That bastard Clem Dredge has her."

Childes lifted bleak eyes to the ruined cabin. "Looks like his work all right."

"My guess is that he came here looking for me, to ask about Dryden. When Loretta told him I was gone, he put two and two together."

"Dredge ain't stupid, boss."

"I put a bullet into him in Old Mexico. I guess he took the rue about that."

"Pity you didn't bed him down, boss."

"Yeah. Pity. My place would be still standing."

"Boss, your arm?"

"I tangled with Dredge in the Madres. Him, or his boys, put a bullet in my side and then shattered my arm."

Pike looked at Childes through the teeming rain. "A right nice feller cut it off for me."

"You look like hell," Childes said. "Skinny as a rail."

"I reckon."

"Let's get you into the bunkhouse where it's dry," Childes said.

"You got coffee?"

"Got that, an' I got some grub."

Pike's sleeve had worked loose and was now flapping in the wind.

"You go on inside, an' I'll take care of your hoss," Childes said.

Pike shook his head. "I'll do that my own self. Just make sure the coffee's on the bile."

He led the dun into the shelter of the pines where there was a patch of good grass and stripped saddle and bridle.

Immeasurably tired, the stump aching, he stowed his rig at the base of a tree and walked back to the bunkhouse.

Childes had coffee waiting.

"Where are the hands, Billy?"

"After I paid them off, they cut a path out of here."

"The herd?"

"Seems fine, boss. I count we still got eighty head, mostly young stuff. We'll make out."

"The money from the army?"

"Six hundred and forty dollars. We can rebuild the ranch and still put in a well."

"Maybe. A one-armed rancher ain't much use to anybody."

"Hell, boss, you'll be a better hand with one arm than most punchers with two, including myself."

Pike spooned sugar into his cup, sitting with his back to the silent, empty bunks. Rain ticked through holes in the roof. "I'm lost, Billy."

Childes nodded. "I can see it hang on you."

"We got hard times coming down."

"What we got right now ain't good, boss. But it will get better."

"When?"

"I don't know."

"Dredge will come back looking for me," Pike said. "If we build, he'll burn it down again."

And that reminded him.

"See anything of Judge Dryden?"

Childes shook his head.

"Sanchez get back?"

"I haven't seen him either."

Pike shivered. He slipped the canvas suspenders off his shoulders, then unbuttoned his wet shirt.

When he removed the shirt, exposing the bandaged stump of his left arm, he heard Childes' sharp intake of breath.

"It ain't pretty, is it, Billy?"

"Boss . . . oh my God . . . boss." Childes buried his face in his hands.

"Still want to work for a one-armed man?"

Without taking his hands from his face, Childes nodded.

Pike smiled. "Billy, you'll do to ride the river with. Any damned day of the week."

Pike lay on his back in a bunk, sleepless, smelling another man's sweat.

Tomorrow he and Billy would take the money from the cattle into town and deposit it in the bank. He knew people there, Maxine among them. Better they see his missing arm, listen to their sympathetic clucks and get the damned thing over with.

After that . . .

There was no after that. As he'd told Billy Childes, he was lost.

It was still raining. Childes snored softly in another bunk. Pike listened into the grumbling night, alert for sounds only he could hear. The thud of a hoof, the triple click of a cocking Colt, the thin whispers of hellbent men.

His stump throbbed. And itched mercilessly. He was bathed in sweat.

He could go after Dredge. Bed him down, as Billy said.

Pike shook his head. No, he had the wrong pig by the tail.

Dredge and his gunmen would open the ball, then dance on his grave.

Over on the other bunk, Childes was muttering in his sleep, drifting through an uneasy dream.

Pike closed his eyes.

In the darkness, he lay unmoving. Like a dead man.

CHAPTER 31

The town lay six miles to the east of the Pecos, in a valley watered by a stream running off the plateau. It had a single street of stores, saloons and warehouses and a roofless theater named the Dixie Gem that had been started three years before and never completed.

After the gold miners packed up and left for richer pickings elsewhere, the town suddenly lost heart and the theater fell by the wayside.

The settlement had a name, Placerville, but, like the Dixie Gem, it had fallen into disfavor and was never used.

It did, however, have the Cattlemen's Bank and Assay Office, a stout, brick building with bars in the windows that had once held off an Apache attack.

Pleased to be getting such a handy deposit, the banker, a pompous man named Taylor, said all the correct, solicitous words about Pike's arm and tut-tutted when he heard what had happened to his ranch.

"An accidental fire, Mr. Pike?" he asked.

"No, it was set deliberately."

"Arson, by God!"

"You could call it that."

"Mr. Pike, as a founding member of the Placerville Vigilance Committee, I will look into this outrage," Taylor said, puffing himself up. "Do you suspect anyone? The greasers are prone to such mischief, you know."

"I think it was done by an outlaw by the name of Clem Dredge," Pike said.

Taylor visibly deflated.

"Ah well, I'll investigate, depend on that." Suddenly he looked like a man in a hurry to go somewhere. "Now I must bid you good day, Mr. Pike. And be assured that your deposit is safe with the Cattlemen's Bank and Assay Office." He fluttered Pike and Childes toward the door. "And oh dear me and I'm so sorry about your arm."

Once outside into the brightening morning, Childes smiled and said: "Why didn't you tell him it was Clem Dredge that took your arm?"

"None of his business," Pike said.

"But hell, a grizzly bear attack?"

"It was all I could come up with," Pike

said. "Let's get breakfast."

The restaurant was busy, but Pike and Childes managed to find a vacant table near the door. They ordered bacon and eggs and a pretty young waitress poured them coffee.

Pike built a cigarette but stilled the match as Childes said: "Well, that's strange."

"What's strange?" Pike said. He lit his smoke.

"Over there by the window, a couple of rannies I know."

Pike was only half interested. "More of your outlaw friends?"

"You could say that."

One of the men glanced over, did a double take on Childes. He leaned over to his companion and said something.

Both men rose and stepped toward Pike's table, bringing their coffee cups with them.

Pike measured them with his eyes. Both were tall, thin as whips and wore their guns as though they'd been born to them.

"Howdy, Billy," the older of the two said. "It's been a spell."

Childes nodded. "A fur piece off your home range, ain't you, Kane?"

"Some." Kane waved to the man at his side. "You remember Dave McMullen?"

"Sure I do," Childes said. He shook Mc-Mullen's hand. "Last I heard, you was do-

206

ing six years in Yuma."

"I surely was. But they let some of the old hands out early on account of a cholera epidemic. Unlucky for some, the cholera. Lucky for me."

The two men sat and Childes introduced Pike.

"Lose that wing in the war, Charlie?" Kane asked.

"No," Pike said.

Kane didn't push it.

"Where you boys headed?" Childes asked into the following silence.

"Waco town," Kane said. "We was told a man's hiring guns and paying top dollar."

Pike's breakfast lay untouched in front of him.

"You have a name for him?" he said.

"Nope," Kane said. "We do what we always do, show up in town and wait for a man to talk to us."

"We ain't never been mistook for drovers," McMullen said.

"Were you told what the job is?" Pike asked.

"Nope," McMullen said, "and we don't much care, so long as it pays well."

Kane's voice held an edge. "You're almighty interested in our doings, Charlie."

Pike backed off. "Could be a range war

brewing," he said. "I'm a rancher and it's good to know these things."

Kane seemed satisfied. "Well, Waco is a ways from here. I'd say you got nothing to worry about."

He rose to his feet. "Real good seeing you again, Billy. And a pleasure to meet you, Charlie."

"You pulling out, Kane?" Childes said.

"Uh-huh. Time is money."

After the men left, Childes said: "Right nice fellers. Me and Kane robbed a bank one time up Wichita way. He did most of the work, but he split the money down the middle, honest and true."

"An upstanding citizen to be sure," Pike said.

He had eaten little, but pushed the plate away from him and lit another cigarette.

"Wonder who's hiring him and Dave," Childes said, the irony in Pike's last statement lost on him.

"I'd guess it's Dredge."

"He need an army to kill one old judge?"

"Dryden's no pushover, Billy."

"You reckon? But still, Kane Towers and Dave McMullen are named men. Dave is good, but Kane's hell on wheels in a fight. He's gunned more than his share."

Childes looked puzzled. "Dredge already

208

has Simpson, Kelly, Mexican Bob and some others and now he's hiring more gunmen to kill a dying old judge? It don't add up, boss."

"Then who's hiring, Billy?"

"I'd guess somebody we don't even know."

"Or somebody we do know," Pike said.

CHAPTER 32

Pike and Childes spent the next two weeks clearing away the debris from the fire.

The cabin had a limestone floor and despite being blackened, had held up to the heat surprisingly well. The fireplace still stood and, as Pike wryly noted: "Now all the place needs is four walls, a chimney, a roof and some furniture."

He tried roping a few times and found he could dab a loop on a steer; if not as well as Childes or any other top hand, at least he didn't look real bad doing it.

Then, at the end of the week, Maxine paid a visit.

Pike was washing up outside the bunkhouse when the woman drove up in a brand-new surrey.

Maxine jumped from the rig and threw herself against Pike.

"Oh, Charlie, I just heard about the arm," she wailed. "You poor, poor thing."

The kiss she laid on him was no more than a sympathetic peck, but her groin grinding against his promised a lot more than mere sympathy.

"How's married life, Maxine?" Pike said, stepping back a little.

"Good, Charlie. Bill Jameson is a hard-working man."

"You weren't pregnant after all, huh?"

"False alarm. But I still thought I was pregnant when Mr. Jameson asked me to marry him. A bird in the hand, Charlie."

"I understand."

"How did it happen?"

"The arm? Grizz, down Old Mexico way."

"Oh, Charlie, that's awful."

"Yeah, awful."

"And then the fire."

"Yeah, then the fire."

"Charlie, there's got to be something I can do for you."

"I'm managing, Maxine."

"To ease your pain. I'll do anything, anything at all."

"Thanks, Maxine. I'll keep that in mind."

"Mr. Jameson is going on a hunting trip next week. He'll be gone for days. I can come over and take care of you."

"I appreciate that, Maxine."

The woman's china doll eyes promised

even more than her groin had.

As Billy Childes told Pike later: "Boss, that bitch was in heat."

But at the time he touched his hat to the woman and said: "Nice to see you again, Maxine."

"You too, Billy."

"We got hot coffee on the stove," Childes said. "Oh, and a barrel of soda crackers."

Pike gave him a look that could have killed a man at twenty paces.

That night a dead gunfighter rode up to the bunkhouse.

Pike was not asleep and he heard the soft footfalls of the horse. They stopped and he listened as the animal tossed its head and rang the bit.

He put on his hat and rose, padding lightly on bare feet. He slipped his Colt from the holster and glanced at Childes. The man was sound asleep, his mouth open, catching flies.

The door creaked open and Pike stepped into darkness.

The horse stood a dozen yards away, a man sitting straight as a poker in the saddle, like a cavalryman on parade.

Behind the black silhouette of horse and rider, a broken sky played hide-and-seek with the stars and a gibbous moon sailed high.

Pike thumbed back the hammer of his revolver, the triple click loud in the stillness.

"I can drill ya, mister," he said.

No answer.

The horse snorted and pawed the ground. A surging wind rustled among the pines and flapped the skirts of the rider's slicker.

Stepping carefully, Pike walked closer.

The tall man on the horse stared straight ahead, ignoring him.

Suddenly Pike was scared; then fear became anger.

"Mister, you start acting real sociable or I'll shoot you right out of the saddle," he said.

The rider said nothing.

His horse turned its head and stared at Pike. It took a couple of steps toward him, then stopped. The moon shrouded itself behind a cloud and the darkness crowded closer.

His temper on a hair trigger since losing his arm, Pike cursed and quickly covered the ground between himself and the rider. He shoved the muzzle of his Colt hard into the man's side, ready to shoot.

It was all it took.

The rider toppled from the saddle and

thudded facedown into the dirt.

Warily, aware of Childes hurrying toward him with a lantern held high, Pike walked around the front of the horse and kneeled behind the fallen man.

"I was asleep, boss, an' I didn't hear you gun him," Childes said.

Bathed in yellow and orange lamplight, Pike shook his head. "I didn't gun him. He was a dead man when he rode in here."

Childes laid the lantern by him, then rolled the man over on his back. He held up the light again.

"Recognize him?" Pike said.

The dead man had a hard, lantern-jawed face, his mouth covered by an untrimmed mustache. He stank of old sweat and newer blood.

"He took three, no, four bullets to the chest," Childes said. "And his gun is gone."

"Recognize him?" Pike asked again.

"I don't know, boss, maybe. When a man's been dead for a spell, his face don't look like it used to look."

"Take a guess."

"He could be Reuben Jody, a hired gun out of San Antone. But it's been a while since I last seen him an' I'm not sure."

Childes scratched under his long johns and said: "Sure looks like ol' Rube, though."

Pike frowned. He studied the crotch of the man's pants and said: "Whoever he is, he's a chest-shot man. So what's all that blood doing down there?"

"Damned if'n I know, boss, unless he was shot in the balls as well."

"Drop his pants, Billy. We'll take a look."

"Don't seem right, boss, doin' that to ol' Rube."

"Do it, Billy."

Childes sighed, shook his head and pulled down the dead man's pants. "Oh my God," he said.

"Somebody gelded him like a hog, didn't they?" Pike said.

"Who would do that?"

"I suspect somebody who wanted information he was unwilling to give," Pike said.

He had thought the man's eyes were closed, but now he pushed back the lids of one, then the other.

Childes stared at Pike. "They've been burned out of his head, boss."

"Looks like."

"A feller might figure he can go on living with no eyes," Childes said. "But cut off his balls and his old man and he'll beg you to kill him."

"You know that from experience, Billy?"

"Nope. It's just what I reckon."

"I'd say you reckon right."

Pike rose to his feet and Childes said: "What's happening, boss?"

It took Pike a few moments to reply. "We're caught in the middle of a war. That's what I think."

He nodded to the man on the ground. "He's one of the first casualties."

"War? Between who?" Childes said.

"Dredge on one side, Henry Dryden on the other."

"An' we're on ol' Hangin' Hank's side, huh?"

"We're on nobody's side, Billy. But I think every man's hand will soon be turned against us."

"Why us?"

"Because we've made some mighty powerful enemies and I don't quite understand why."

"Know what I wish, boss?"

"Tell me."

"I wish to hell Pete Sanchez was back."

"That makes two of us," Pike said.

CHAPTER 33

Pike and Childes buried the dead gunman at first light.

Billy figured it was within his rights to confiscate the man's horse and add it to the remuda.

"Serves him right fer showin' up here dead as a wooden Indian," he said.

Maxine drove into the ranch early that afternoon.

But this time she was more horrified than horny.

"Charlie, I was in school yesterday and two men called me out," she said, her voice small, tight and breathless.

Childes poured the woman coffee.

"What did they want?" Pike said.

"You."

"Did they ask you where I was?"

"They know where you are, Charlie."

"Did you recognize them?"

"Never seen them before. They were both

big, rough-looking men, carrying guns."

Maxine swallowed hard. "They scared me, Charlie."

She reached into the pocket of her dress. "They gave me this for you."

Pike took the folded note from Maxine's hand and read: KUM INTO TOWN TER-MORRA. OR WE'LL KUM AFTER YOU.

"This was all," Pike said. He passed the note to Childes.

"Just that. And they said they'd be waiting for you at the Alamo." Maxine's brow wrinkled. "They mean to kill you, Charlie."

Her coffee untouched, she rose to her feet. "I want out. Please forget you ever knew me, Charlie."

She rushed out the door, but Pike caught up and walked her to her rig. "I'll sure miss you, Maxine," he said.

"Maybe so, Charlie, but I like my men alive. And with two arms."

"Bitch," Childes said as he watched the woman drive away.

"She's scared, Billy," Pike said. "Just plain scared."

"Hell, ain't we all, boss?"

Pike rubbed the itching stump of his arm and felt the desolate emptiness of his shirtsleeve.

"Billy," he said, "I'm sick and tired of being scared. A man can't live like this."

"What does a man do?" Childes said.

"He meets what's scaring him head-on."

"You mean meet them two hard cases in town?"

"Just that. They could be Dredge and Simpson. Maybe I can get it over with."

"Boss, you don't have the gun savvy for that, no offense."

"None taken."

"Then let's lay for them here. We can hide up and blast 'em when they get close."

"That's a way, Charlie, but it's not going to be my way. Besides, I tried bushwhacking before and all it did was lose me an arm."

"Well, I'm coming with you, boss. I'm pretty handy with the iron."

"I'll do it alone, Billy."

"Don't be a hero, boss. You ain't Wild Bill Hickok."

Normally Pike would have smiled at that, but this time he did not.

"Right now I feel like half a man, Billy."

"The arm?"

"That and being scared all the time, the way I am."

"Getting kilt by a couple of Dredge's hard cases ain't going to make you feel any better."

"Then I'll die on my own terms. Standing up with a gun in my hand."

"Charlie," Childes said, using Pike's given name, a rare thing for him, "you talk about being half a man. Well, if I was half of the half of a man you think you are, I'd be mighty content."

This time Pike smiled. "If I fall, the ranch is yours. All I ask is six feet of it."

"If you fall, boss, I swear — I'll lay Dredge at your feet."

Pike waited until the sun dropped lower in the western sky before he saddled the dun.

Some gunfighters — high-strung, passionate men like Hickok and Holliday — got likkered up before a fight. Others — ice-cold killers like Earp and Hardin — did not.

Pike hoped the two men waiting for him in town were of the hot-blooded variety. If the gunmen had been drinking, it could provide him with the split-second edge he needed.

"I wish you'd let me go with you, boss," Childes said.

"I need you here at the ranch, Billy," Pike said.

Childes gouged dirt with the toe of his boot. "I cleaned and oiled your Colt. Chose the shells my own self, made sure the lead is seated properly."

Pike nodded. "Thank you kindly."

Childes' talking was done. Nothing else he could say would change things. He gave Pike his hand. "Good luck, boss."

Pike shook, touched his hat to his foreman and rode out.

He didn't look back. At Childes or the ruin of his ranch.

CHAPTER 34

Charlie Pike rode east under a violet sky ribboned with scarlet and jade. The air smelled of pine and sage, the breeze soft as a sleeping woman's breath.

It was midweek and the town was quiet, the saloons blazing with light but with few patrons inside. The stores were still open, their windows glowing orange in the gathering dark and the dress shop where Loretta had bought her clothes had customers inside.

Pike rode past the Lone Star, where someone, probably a bored saloon girl, was picking out the notes of a Chopin nocturne with one finger.

The Alamo lay just ahead of him, four ponies at the hitching rail.

Pike climbed from the saddle, glanced at the night sky and stepped into the saloon.

There were half a dozen men inside, four at the bar and two sitting at a table, sharing a bottle. A small brunette in a lavender silk dress stood at the end of the bar, talking to the bartender.

Pike sized up the patrons quickly; then his eyes settled on the two at the table.

They were not Dredge and Simpson, but had to be the men he was looking for.

Both wore slickers, sported dragoon mustaches trimmed in the latest handlebar fashion and both looked tough and capable.

They were what they were, gun-carrying men who would kill for a price.

Pike strolled to the table and the men looked up at him. They measured him from head to toe, settling at last on the empty sleeve of his shirt.

"What the hell do you want?" one of them asked.

"I heard you're looking for me," Pike said.

He took the note from his shirt pocket, opened it and laid it on the table front of the two gunmen.

"Which one of you illiterates wrote that?" Pike said.

Sitting down, the two men knew they were at a disadvantage. They looked at Pike, seeking an edge.

He gave them none.

He pushed against the table with his groin, forcing it against the gunmen, a move they didn't like.

The saloon was so quiet, he could hear the tick of the railroad clock on the wall. A man left the bar and, on his toes, walked out of the saloon.

Pike picked up the bottle from the table, but with his thumb down, as he would hold a club.

"Who's paying you to kill me?" he asked. "That piece of human garbage, Clem Dredge?"

An armed man, good with the iron he carries, can only be pushed so far. Gunfighter pride will drive him to make a play.

"Damn you!" the man on the left yelled. He slammed back his chair and started to rise, his hand streaking for the gun at his waist.

Pike did two things very fast.

He smashed the whiskey bottle on the table and in one smooth motion shoved the jagged end into the gunman's face.

Outraged, the man bellowed in pain and staggered back.

The gunman on Pike's right had been shocked by the sudden savagery of Pike's attack. He had not expected such from a one-armed drover.

But now he was on his feet, clawing for his gun.

The man's draw was smooth and fast, Pike's a split second slower . . . a moment of time, but the difference between life and death in a gunfight.

The gunman fired.

His bullet tugged at Pike's empty sleeve, jerking it from his belt.

Pike's shot was better. Hit low in the belly, the gunman half turned and slammed against the wall, out of it for now.

His face a scarlet mask, the other man wiped blinding blood from his eyes and fired at Pike. A miss.

Pike fired.

His bullet hit the gunman in the chest and staggered him. Pike fired again. This time the man went down.

The gut-shot gunman was hit hard but game. He pushed off the wall, his gun coming up fast.

A shotgun blast from the bar hit him again in the belly, nearly cutting him in half. The man screamed and went down.

Pike turned. The bartender was lowering a smoking Greener.

"I don't like strangers killing my cash-paying regulars," the man said. "I can't abide it and I won't stand for it."

Pike let his Colt hang by his side. The man who'd been hit twice in the gut was dead.

He had no need to look at him to tell that.

The second gunman was barely alive, clinging desperately to the life ebbing out of him.

Suddenly sick of the whole thing, Pike said: "Take your medicine, old fellow."

The man either tried to smile or grimaced in pain, Pike could never say which. "You've killed me, you bastard."

"You gave me no choice," Pike said.

"The gold is safe, Pike," the gunman said. "Hid away. Damn you, you crippled son of a bitch, you'll never get your dirty paw on it."

Then he made a noise deep in his throat and died.

Pike looked at the bartender. "What gold was he talking about?"

The man shook his head. "Beats the hell out of me."

He opened the Greener and, with steady fingers, removed the spent shells.

It was the cool, collected action of a man who had killed before.

CHAPTER 35

"Gold? What gold?"

"Beats me, Billy," Pike said.

"You sure that's what the son of a bitch said?"

"Dead sure."

Childes took off his hat and scratched his head. "Well, doesn't that beat all?"

"He said the gold was hidden where I'd never find it," Pike said. "Hell, I'm not even looking for it."

"Wherever it is."

"Yeah, wherever it is."

"Boss, I figured you were a dead man fer certain."

Pike smiled. "So did I. The bartender — what's his name?"

"Matt Wilder."

"Yeah, him. He shot one of those rannies off of me. Cut him in half with a Greener scattergun."

"Why did he throw in with you?"

"Said he couldn't afford to lose a cash customer."

"Wilder would say that. He was a lawman at one time, you know. Worked for ol' Judge Parker up in the Indian Territory."

"He saved my ass."

Pike and Childes sat outside the bunkhouse in the cool evening. They were passing a bottle of rye back and forth, a drink Pike needed badly.

"Tell me about the gunfight again, boss," Childes said.

"I done told you already."

"The bit about you smashing the bottle. I would never have thought o' that."

"It isn't an easy thing to shove a broken bottle into a man's face."

"Then why did you?"

"I didn't have time to do anything else."

Childes opened his mouth to speak, but Pike said: "Coyotes coming in close."

"Well, we don't have calves on the ground."

Pike listened into the night, then said: "A hunting pair."

"I reckon so. Now about the fight, I —"

"Dredge hired those men," Pike said. His talk about the gunfight was over. "He wants me dead, but didn't have the inclination to do it himself. Why?"

"He's a wanted man, boss."

"That's never stopped him before."

Pike drank from the bottle, then said: "Maybe he didn't have the time."

"Real busy burying his gold so you wouldn't find it, huh?"

"That might be closer to the truth than you think, Billy."

"Hell, I was only joking."

"The man I killed wasn't. I think Dredge is running scared."

Childes laughed. "Boss, Clem Dredge don't scare worth a damn."

"He has gold hidden someplace and he figures I know about it and want it. That scares him."

"But why you?"

"Because he thinks I'm working for Henry Dryden. For some reason, Dryden has put the fear of God into him."

"Hell, you really think Clem is afeared of a sick old man?"

"Dryden is not that old and I don't think he's sick. I've seen him shoot and he's good with a gun. Maybe better than most. He could be dangerous."

"So you reckon Hangin' Hank his own self is after Dredge's gold?"

"Maybe."

"Well, boss, all I hear is a heap of maybes.

The man who told you about the gold was dying. I've heard dying men say strange things."

Pike rose to his feet. "We'd better turn in, Billy. We got some work to do tomorrow. I want to start rebuilding the ranch house."

Childes said: "Good, boss. Then maybe we can get back to the way we was before the old man's letter came."

"Billy, we'll never get back to the way we was before the old man's letter came," Pike said.

Pike rousted Childes out of his bunk before daybreak, then ignored the man as he groused and grumbled his way through breakfast.

There was no heavy timber for the taking on the Stockton Plateau. But as Childes drank his fourth cup of coffee and smoked his fifth cigarette of the day, he felt civil enough to agree with Pike that they should go into town and buy sawn lumber.

"Nothing wrong with a board house," Childes said. "So long as a man don't get one o' them nor'easter blizzards."

"Ain't likely in this neck of the woods," Pike said.

"No, it ain't likely." Childes stilled in his chair, his cigarette dangling from his lips.

"We got comp'ny, boss."

"Maxine?"

"Like hell. Look outside."

Pike stepped to the window.

Twelve men in columns of twos were riding toward the bunkhouse.

"Damn him," Pike said. "Damn him to hell."

Childes was beside him. "Who is it?"

"Judge Henry Dryden," Pike said.

CHAPTER 36

The column halted, then deployed into line.

Pike and Childes stepped outside.

"Howdy, Kane, Dave," Childes said. "I see you found the feller you was looking fer."

"Reckon so, Billy," Kane Towers said.

Dryden kneed his horse forward. He looked younger, stronger, sitting his saddle with all the pride and arrogance of a Confederate cavalry officer.

"Good to see you again, Major Pike," Dryden said.

"It's Charlie, or have you forgotten?" Pike said.

"Very well — Charlie," Dryden said.

His eyes roamed over the leveled ranch house. "Dredge?"

"I reckon."

"All the more reason for you to return to duty. I want you to ride with me again, Charlie."

"Dryden, I don't owe you a damned thing," Pike said.

"Your life doesn't count?"

"You didn't save my life. Some Irish sergeant did. I know it now and you've known it all along."

"Ah, but he was under my command, wasn't he?"

Dryden waved a dismissive hand. "But all that doesn't matter. I want Clem Dredge and I need you to help me find him."

"You got eleven hard cases backing you, Dryden. You don't need a one-armed man."

"Thirteen hard cases in fact. I have a couple more back there somewhere with the pack mules."

"You haven't told me why you want me."

"These men are mercenaries, Charlie. They fight for money. I need a man with your loyalty. I can't tell you why now, but all will become clear later."

"Go to hell, Dryden," Pike said.

"You heard the boss, beat it," Childes said. He stood at Pike's side, wearing his gun. Tense and ready.

Kane Towers leaned forward in the saddle. "Billy, you're a friend. I don't like gunning my friends."

"Then tell your boss he's not welcome here," said Childes.

"Stay out of this, Billy, it's my fight," Pike said.

"Boss, that's a hell of a thing to say to me," Childes said.

"Listen to him, Billy," Towers said. "I don't want to kill you."

The gunfighter's face was empty, but his eyes glowed with blue fire.

"Enough of this!" Dryden said. "I want no gunplay."

He turned in the saddle. "Mr. Towers, go tell Mr. Greer to bring in the whore. Quickly now."

Towers gave Childes a last, lingering look, then said: "Anything you say, Judge."

After Towers left, Dryden lifted his great beak of a nose. "I smell coffee, Charlie. Can you spare a cup?"

Unwilling to break a lifetime habit of hospitality, Pike nodded. "Light and set."

"Thank you, Charlie," Dryden said. He turned to his men. "Stand down for now."

Dryden swung out of the saddle and walked toward the bunkhouse.

Billy Childes watched his every step, fuming.

Taking a seat at the table, Dryden picked up a cup and motioned with it to Childes, smiling. "Will you be mother, Billy?"

"You go to hell," Childes said.

"Billy, step outside," Pike said.

"Let me put a bullet into him, boss, end this thing."

"He's under my roof, Billy," Pike said. He picked up the coffeepot. "Please, go outside."

Childes stormed out and Dryden said: "A hot-tempered young man."

"He rides for the brand," Pike said.

Dryden nodded. "And from what I could see when I rode in, a fine brand it is."

Pike let that go and began to build himself a cigarette.

"Good coffee, Charlie," Dryden said. He glanced at the tobacco and papers in Pike's hand. "You do that very well for a one-armed man."

"I manage."

"You disappoint me, Charlie," Dryden said. "When I rode up I expected the hand of friendship. But I was met with hostility and threats of violence."

He motioned with his head to Pike's empty sleeve. "You haven't even told me how you lost that, as one friend to another."

"You're not my friend, Dryden."

"Ah, yet another disappointment."

"It's the way it shakes out," Pike said.

"The arm?"

"Clem Dredge. It happened in a fight

across the Rio Bravo. You don't need to know more than that."

"So you have yet another reason to hate the man."

"Seems like."

"And you were in Mexico on my behalf, I assume. I'm touched, touched to the quick."

Dryden took a slim black cigar from the pocket of his coat. "I plan to make you a rich man, Charlie."

He lit the cigar.

From behind a blue cloud of smoke, he said: "You'll be richer beyond anything you can imagine."

"You're talking about Dredge's hidden gold."

Dryden was surprised. "How did you know about that?"

"A dying man told me. He said I'd never find it."

Dredge nodded. "One of the men you killed in the Alamo last night."

"You heard about that?"

"Yes."

"Dredge sent them after me. He thinks I'm working for you."

"And you will be, Charlie. Depend on it, you will be." Dryden shrugged. "Or you'll be dead."

"Boss, you better come out here."

Childes stood at the door, his face showing both anger and strain.

Pike rose and stepped outside.

Dryden stood beside him. He held his cigar between two fingers and thumb and studiously flicked off ash with his pinkie.

"I'm sure you remember Miss Loretta Lamont," he said.

CHAPTER 37

Loretta, her dress stained, roughly torn away from her shoulders, stood among Dryden's men.

She had a bruise on her left cheekbone and a deep cut on her bottom lip. Her face was pale, her eyes wide, tired and frightened.

"I'll take her inside," Pike said. "She needs rest."

"No, you won't, Charlie," Dryden said.

"Why not?"

"She's my bargaining chip," Dryden said.

"I don't bargain with the devil," Pike said.

"That will be too bad, Charlie. Bad for you, bad for the whore."

Pike stared at Loretta, a slight, frail figure among Dryden's burly gunmen.

"Charlie, you will agree to ride with me, or —"

"Don't listen to him, Charlie," Loretta yelled. "He'll kill —"

A man standing beside the woman back-handed her hard across the face. She fell to the ground, blood scarlet in her mouth.

"Or I'll hang the whore," Dryden said calmly, as though nothing had happened.

He motioned forward Towers and another man. "Disarm them."

As rifles were trained on Pike and Childes, Towers relieved them of their guns.

To Childes, Towers said: "Sorry, Billy."

"Go to hell, Kane," Childes said.

"Now, Charlie, I know you don't like to see women abused and you certainly don't enjoy hangings. Very soon you will witness both. Unless of course —"

"She means nothing to me," Pike said.

He was trying to run a bluff with a busted flush, knowing it would not force Dryden to throw in his hand.

"Very well, then."

Dryden stepped toward his gunmen. "You men, take the woman into the bunkhouse and rape her until she screams for mercy. Then rape her some more. After you're done, bring out what's left of her and hang her from the cottonwood over yonder."

That did not sit well with several of the more professional gunmen, including Kane Towers and Dave McMullen. They were outraged, their mouths tight and grim under their mustaches.

But there were more than enough grinning border trash willing to do what Dryden had ordered.

Half a dozen picked up Loretta and dragged her, kicking and screaming, toward the bunkhouse.

"Judge, this ain't right," Towers said.

"You don't like it, Mr. Towers?"

"No, sir, I don't." He drew his gun. "And I'm going to put a stop to it."

Suddenly Dryden's Colt was in his hand. He fired once and Towers fell. He was dead when he hit the ground, a hole in the middle of his forehead leaking blood and brain.

His gun trailing smoke, in a lethal whisper Dryden said: "Is there anyone else who doesn't like it? You perhaps, Mr. McMullen?"

The speed of Dryden's draw had surprised everyone. Even the lowlifes dragging Loretta into the bunkhouse had stopped at the door, their jaws sagging.

"I got no objections," McMullen said, the words threatening to strangle him.

"Good," Dryden said after a cold silence. "I'm glad you're not as high-strung and traitorous as your friend."

From over at the bunkhouse Loretta

yelled: "Leave me the hell alone, you animals!"

Dryden looked over that way and nodded. Loretta was dragged inside.

"Wait!" Pike said. "All right, Dryden, you win. Let the woman go."

"You will ride with me, Charlie?"

"Yes."

"On your word of honor as an officer and a gentleman?"

"Yeah, on my word of honor. Now let Loretta go, you black-hearted bastard."

"McMullen," Dryden said. "Stop them. Bring them out there."

He looked at Pike. "I'm glad you've had a change of heart, Charlie. Now we are perfect friends once again."

"I'm not your friend, Dryden," Pike said.

"Animals! You perverted sons of bitches!" Loretta yelled as she was pushed outside.

Pike was strangely pleased to hear her air out her lungs again.

"Charlie, have you ever heard of a town in Mexico called Vamoose Gulch?"

"Heard of it," Pike said. "It's a legend."

Dryden leaned back in his chair and studied the end of his cigar. "It's no legend. It exists."

"If that was true, the Mexican *federales*

would have wiped it off the map years ago."

Dryden poured himself more coffee, then said: "A town run by outlaws for outlaws is not an easy nut to crack, Charlie."

"You think that's where Dredge is?" Pike said.

"I know that's where he is," Dryden said.

"Somebody's shooting you a line of bullshit. There's no such town."

"Why won't the Texas Rangers ride west of Eagle Pass, Charlie?"

"Because it's Mexican territory."

"No, it's because of Vamoose Gulch."

Pike glanced at Childes. "Any of your outlaw friends ever mention it, Billy?"

Childes looked uncomfortable, unwilling to agree with Dryden for any reason.

"Well?" Pike said.

"Remember Winton Heath, stayed with us for a couple of days back in 'seventy-eight?"

"No."

"Well, Wint told me him and three of his boys spent a spring in Vamoose Gulch after they robbed a Kansas Pacific cannonball."

"Was he spinning a big windy?" Pike said.

"Not Wint, not his style."

"What did he say about the town, Billy?" Dryden said.

Childes answered the question, but looked at Pike, as though it had come from him.

"Wint says there were maybe sixty, seventy hard cases in town that spring, but it's a right peaceful place. The vigilantes are all retired outlaws and they ain't shy about hanging a man if he steps over the line."

Pike's eyes shifted to Dryden.

"Don't seem like Clem Dredge's kind of burg," he said.

"He's on the dodge from both the law and me," Dryden said. "So long as he thinks he's being protected, he'll behave himself."

"You plan on just riding into an outlaw town and killing one of their own?" Pike said.

"Oh dear no, Charlie, you have it all wrong."

"Then what do you plan?"

"To talk to Mr. Dredge."

"Talk?"

"Yes, him and us, very civil-like."

"I'll ask you again: Why do you need me?"

"I want you to join in the conversation, Charlie. Your presence at our meeting will be most important. Vital, you might say."

Chapter 38

"I seem to keep asking you this, boss, but let me go with you," Childes said.

Pike had thrown his saddle on the dun, refused help from Childes and now he tightened the cinch with one hand. "I need you here, Billy."

"Why, for God's sake?"

"Well, for one thing, go into town and order lumber for the cabin. If it arrives before I get back, take money out of the bank and pay for it."

"That's it?"

"I'm sure you can find other chores to keep yourself busy around here."

Childes was quiet, arranging words in his mind. Then he said: "Hangin' Hank looks like a lawman."

Pike was surprised. "You think so? All duded up in a frock coat and top hat, he looks more like a five-ace gambler to me."

"He was a judge, boss. The stink of the

law still hangs on him like flies on shit."

The zebra dun was up on its toes, tossing its head, eager for the trail.

"An' he's a killer, boss. That stink hangs on him as well."

"You're talking about Vamoose Gulch, huh?" Pike said.

"Lawman and killer. It's a bad combination in that town."

"In any town," Pike said.

"Now take a minute and hear me out," Childes said. "Say I ride ahead and hole up in the hills somewhere an' lay for Dryden? I can shoot him out of the saddle and our problem is solved."

"Suppose you miss?"

"I don't miss too often with a Winchester."

"I told you before, Billy, it's not the way."

Pike smiled. "Besides, Dryden said he'd make me rich."

"You want to be rich, boss?"

"Doesn't everybody? Six hundred dollars doesn't go far when a man's trying to build a ranch."

"I say we gun him now."

"Let Dryden play out his hand. After that, we'll talk about gunning him."

"You could be dead by then, boss."

"If I am, kill him," Pike said. "How does that set with you?"

"Sets with me just fine. But I think you're making a big mistake. An' riding into Vamoose Gulch with Henry Dryden will be another."

Dryden led out his men thirty minutes later.

Pike took up the rear, riding just ahead of the pack mules.

After a couple of miles, Loretta drifted back and rode beside him.

"Sorry about the arm, Charlie," she said. "I heard Dryden say Clem Dredge did it."

"Him or one of his boys."

Pike rode in silence for a few moments, then said: "Now he owes me for an arm and my ranch house." He nodded. "And for a two-holer outhouse, the only one like it in the damned county."

"Dredge didn't burn your ranch, Charlie."

Pike's head swung in her direction.

"It was Dryden," Loretta said. "He wanted to give you another reason to hate Dredge. A little insurance, you might say."

Pike felt as if he'd been punched in the gut.

The morning was bright and Dryden set a fast pace, putting distance behind them. Before noon they would cross the Rio Bravo into Mexico.

Through the dust cloud, Pike made out the judge's skinny back. He was suddenly aware of the Colt on his hip. One shot. Just one aimed shot.

"Forget it, Charlie," Loretta said, reading Pike's blazing eyes and the stiff jut of his jaw. "You'd be a dead man a second later."

"He lied to me, damn him. Burned me out and blamed it on Dredge."

"Since when does Henry Dryden tell the truth to anybody?"

Loretta opened the battered parasol she'd somehow managed to preserve through all that had happened to her and held it over her head.

"Henry's men dragged me out before they torched the place," she said. "I never did get to finish *The Fair Maid of Perth.* Does she marry the guy in the end?"

"I saved the book," Pike said. "It's a bit scorched, but you'll be able to finish it when you get back to the ranch."

"I'm going back to the ranch?"

"Unless you have a better place in mind."

"No, it will do for now."

Loretta thought about that. "I may be a whore, but I'm not bedding down in the bunkhouse with two horny punchers. I'd never get any sleep."

Pike laughed, his first in a while, and, if only for a moment, it felt just fine.

CHAPTER 39

They crossed the Rio Bravo, then followed the river to the southeast, heading in the general direction of Eagle Pass.

Dryden sent out a couple of scouts ahead of his line of march, aware that Apaches often raided into that part of Mexico.

There was no joshing or laughter among the men.

They rode slumped in the saddle, silent, Dryden's cold-blooded murder of Kane Towers weighing on them.

So far, it had been a sullen and bitter ride.

The only loyalty such men offered an employer was what little could be bought with money.

But Towers had been a gun-for-hire like themselves. They depended on each other for survival and his killing rankled.

Pike looked around him at the grim, unsmiling faces. They were professional gunmen, ruthless, ugly in spirit, hard men who knew the way of the Colt and killed freely and often.

But if it came down to it, would they fight for Dryden on grounds of his choosing? And if they did, would they stand?

Pike had questions without answers.

Only time would tell.

That night they made brooding camp in a shallow arroyo in the thinly forested hill country north of the San Rodrigo River.

The men were ill-tempered, short with one another and once Dryden had to step between two of them with gun drawn. The argument, over a tin cup, would have ended with lighthearted banter in a cheerful camp, but quickly blew out of all proportion in this one.

Exerting his authority, Dryden sent out a couple of pickets, reminding them this was Apache country. He also warned them that Clem Dredge was not a man to sit back and let things happen.

In that, as Pike would recall later, Dryden was a prophet.

"You can see why I need you, Charlie," Dryden said.

He sat beside Pike and laid his coffee cup between his skinny, booted legs.

"This rabble is not to be trusted, not for a

moment."

Pike smiled. "If they decide to come after you, Dryden, I won't stand at your side."

"Not even for as much gold as you can carry?" Dryden said. "And I mean when you had two arms."

Dryden lit a cigar. "Besides, they won't come after me. If they kill me they won't get paid and they know that."

"They'll just take the money off your cold, stiff carcass, Dryden," Pike said, smiling, enjoying himself.

"I thought about that, even before this enterprise started. I won't pay them from my strongbox. My agent in Waco will settle accounts when the job is done. I will give each man a receipt with the amount to be paid to him."

Pike built a cigarette. "Thought of everything, haven't you?"

"I believe so."

"Have you thought about what you're going to do if Clem Dredge doesn't want to talk to you? As far as I can tell, he ain't a talking man."

"I'll make him talk to me."

"How do you plan on doing that?"

"Ah, so glad you asked." Dryden's eyes wandered over the camp, then to the glowing tip of his cigar. "I have an . . . ah . . . associate who will join us in Vamoose Gulch."

He turned and looked at Pike, his eyes pools of shadow. "The man is very good at what he does. Quite mad, of course, but he'll get Dredge to talk to me."

"Does he have a name?"

"Yes, but what he's called doesn't matter."

"How did you hook up with him, Dryden?"

"When I was a judge, he came in very handy."

"How so?"

"Well, when I was determined to hang a man, a confession made it all so much easier."

"And the madman got it for you."

"Precisely."

"How many men did you send to the gallows after a forced confession?"

"Many. The exact number isn't important." He waved his cigar, taking in the men around the campfire. "Scum like these are not sorely missed, except by whores like Loretta."

Dryden grinned. "Look at her, sitting over there showing her legs, wearing those ankle boots. Only a whore wears boots with high heels like that."

He shook his head. "I should let the men

have at her, cheer them up some."

"Dryden," Pike said sociably, as though he was talking to kinfolk, "do that and I'll kill you."

Dryden's smile was slight. "You know, Charlie, I believe you would. Or you'd try at least."

He turned his head. "You love the bitch. I had no idea."

"I don't love her. But I won't see her abused or manhandled."

"There speaks the true Southern officer and gentleman."

"How the hell would you know, Dryden?" Pike said.

Whatever Dryden was about to say was lost in the shout and bubbling shriek that came from the mouth of the arroyo.

CHAPTER 40

Men were on their feet, guns drawn, staring into the echoing darkness.

"Was it Clyde?" Dryden ran to the fire. "Was that Lucian Clyde?"

"Sure as hell sounded like him," a man said.

"Gladhorn is with him," Dryden said.

He stepped away from the fire and cupped both hands to his mouth. "Clyde, Gladhorn, are you there?"

The answering silence mocked him.

Dryden turned, drawing his gun. "You men, come with me."

Pike rose to his feet, adjusted the hang of his holster and went in search of the gunmen who had followed Dryden into the gloom.

They were not hard to find.

Dryden and the others clustered around the sprawled bodies of Clyde and Gladhorn at the mouth of the arroyo.

Pike glanced at the dead men. Clyde's throat had been cut. Gladhorn had a wound in his chest, no doubt made by the same knife that had done for his partner.

He looked at Dryden. "Got yourself a problem, Henry," he said.

Dryden's cold eyes spiked at him. "Who did this? Apaches?"

"Apaches don't wear boots." This from Dave McMullen, who had scouted the ground. "Boot tracks all over the place."

"I'd say it was one of Dredge's men," Pike said. "My guess would be Mexican Bob and that he was led here by a tracker named McCone. Bob's been around some and he's probably fit Apaches in the past. They taught him how to crawl up on a man."

"Are you telling me that Dredge knows we're here?" Dryden said.

"He knows," Pike said. "McCone's probably been tracking us since we crossed the Rio Bravo."

"And maybe you sent that hand of yours on ahead to tell Dredge."

A towhead with ugly eyes was staring hard at Pike. "Man on a fast horse could have done that."

Pike let his own eyes empty. "A mighty fast horse."

The towhead looked at Dryden. "Judge, I

say a one-armed man is bad luck on the trail, especially one in cahoots with Dredge. I say we get rid of him."

"That's my decision to make, not yours, Tate." Dryden looked around at his men. "We'll bury our dead at first light."

He waved in the direction of the camp. "There's a jug in one of the packs. Share it among you."

The man called Tate threw Pike a look of dislike. "This ain't over."

"Until it's over," Pike said.

None of Dryden's men were the sort to scare easily. But the killing of Towers and the savage deaths of Clyde and Gladhorn had unsettled them and they hit the whiskey hard.

Pike saw the trouble coming from a ways off.

He saw anger build in Cletus Tate with every pull from the jug. The man was looking to blame someone, anyone, for three deaths he'd been unable to foresee or prevent.

And he was afraid.

A scared man, close kin to a coward with a gun, can be the most dangerous creature on earth.

Pike sat with Loretta. The moon had

spiked itself on a pine and a thin, opal mist shrouded the ground. Among the foothills, coyotes talked to the night.

"I would like to have lived in those days," Loretta said.

"What days?" Pike said. He was watching Tate, who had gotten to his feet.

"The *Fair Maid of Perth* days," Loretta said. "What is it they're called?"

"The Middle Ages," Pike said.

"Yeah, that's it, the Middle Ages, when men were gallant knights and women were ladies."

"And the only person who wasn't covered in shit was the king," Pike said.

Tate was stepping toward him.

"That's right, Charlie. Shatter my illusions. I bet —"

Loretta looked up at Tate, her eyes questioning.

The man ignored her. He kicked the sole of Pike's boot. "You, get on your feet."

Pike took the makings from his shirt pocket and began to build a smoke. He didn't look at Tate.

The gunman reached down and slapped paper and tobacco from Pike's hand. "Saddle up," Tate said. "You're leaving."

Pike felt irritation, not anger. "And if I don't feel like leaving?"

"Then I'll whale the tar out of you and put you on your horse myself."

The line was drawn.

Pike looked over at Dryden, expecting him to intervene. But the man was sitting by the fire, smoking a cigar. He had an amused smile on his lips, as though he was enjoying the show.

There was a sadistic streak in Dryden that Pike had recognized before. He would do nothing — at least until he saw how this played out.

"Leave him alone, you bastard," Loretta said. "He's only got one arm."

"His bad luck," Tate said.

"One arm or no," Pike said, "the day will never come that I can't beat a sorry piece of trash like you."

"Get on your damned feet and prove it," Tate said.

"Take your gun off, Clete," a man said. "We don't want another killing here."

Tate unbuckled his gun belt, let it drop, then stepped back as Pike got to his feet.

Pike's own gun thudded to the ground.

"Now we're even," he said, smiling.

Tate swung a powerful roundhouse right.

Charlie Pike had learned about skull, boot and fist fighting from his drunken old man. From the time he was fourteen, his father had attacked him as he'd tried to protect his ma. By Pike's reckoning, the man had beaten him to a bloody pulp one hundred and twenty-eight times. On the one-hundred-and-twenty-ninth time, seventeen and almost man-grown into height and hard muscle, Pike was the one who beat his pa into a bloody pulp.

His old man had never tackled him again.

Tate did not know these things, but it would have been better for him if he had.

Pike turned his head at the last moment and Tate's knuckles only grazed his cheekbone, drawing blood, but it was not a knockout blow. The man was off balance for a second and Pike stepped inside and lifted him with an uppercut to the chin.

Tate went down hard, but tried to gather himself, getting to his hands and knees, shaking blood from his bitten tongue.

Moving in again, Pike slammed a kick into Tate's ribs, then another. The big towhead groaned and rolled over on his right side.

Pike took a step back, letting Tate slowly climb to his feet.

"Fight fair, Pike," somebody yelled.

"He's only got one arm," Loretta screamed. "He doesn't need to play by the damn rules."

Tate bored in again, swinging.

The man's right missed Pike, but Tate's left nailed him squarely on the jaw. Hit hard, Pike fell on his back, his stump taking most of the impact.

As pain spiked at him and the night cart-wheeled around him, Pike saw Tate get himself set. The heel of the man's right boot came down fast, trying to smash Pike's face.

Pike rolled and the boot missed his head by a fraction of an inch. Off balance again, Tate was vulnerable. Pike kicked out at the towhead's left knee. The man's leg buckled and he fell on his back.

Tate's legs were open and Pike drove the toe of his boot into his crotch. Tate screamed and clutched at himself, grimacing in pain.

Again Pike stepped back.

He waited until Tate staggered to his feet, then stepped in quickly.

Grabbing the towhead by his shirtfront, Pike jerked him toward him. Driven by all the force of his shoulder and neck muscles, Pike slammed the top of his forehead into the bridge of Tate's nose.

Everyone in camp heard the bones splinter.

Blood streaming over his mouth and down his chin, Tate stepped back. He didn't like what Pike was giving him and it showed in his wary eyes.

Tate swung a weak, ineffective right that Pike took on his shoulder. He walked in on the towhead and slammed a straight right into the man's face. Tate lowered his guard and Pike hit him again, dropping him.

The big towhead was as game as they come and tried to get to his feet. But he looked up at Pike standing bloody and terrible above him and lifted his left arm in surrender.

"Huzzah for the man from Texas!" Loretta yelled.

But there was no response from the men who had stood to watch the fight.

Finally Dryden said: "One of you men help Tate to his feet."

"Ain't much of him left to help," Dave McMullen said.

Pike worked the bruised fingers of his hand. He felt good. Almost as good as the day he whipped his pa.

CHAPTER 41

The sign alongside the wagon road leading into Vamoose Gulch left no doubt about the town's sentiments.

Attention all bunko artists, goldbrickers, short-card artists, dance hall loungers, thieves and tramps ~ stay out or get hung.

Pike turned to Dryden, grinning. "Kinda lets you out, don't it, Henry?"

"Charlie, do not presume on my friendship too much," Dryden said. "That could be a dangerous mistake."

Pike had expected a town run by outlaws for outlaws to be a tumbledown hellhole that served up dead men for breakfast every morning.

But Vamoose Gulch was a Western settlement like any other.

Early as it was, there were men and

women on the street. Careful-eyed outlaws and gunmen rubbed shoulders with businessmen in broadcloth and saloon girls on their way to bed talked with respectable matrons in sunbonnets, shopping baskets over their arms.

The town was neat, clean, painted, the only discordant sounds the clang of iron from the blacksmith's shop and the lumberyard's whining ripsaw.

A stage unloaded passengers at the express office and to Pike's surprise a whitewashed church stood at the end of the street.

Dryden threaded his way through people and loaded freight wagons, then raised his hand, halting the column outside the Cactus Belle Saloon.

He turned in the saddle. "This place will be my headquarters. Mr. McMullen, detail a couple of men to take the horses to the livery."

Loretta's eyes were on the church. She pushed her paint in that direction.

Dryden swung out of the saddle. Then Pike and the others followed him inside.

There was only one early drinker in the saloon, a gray-haired businessman drinking coffee at a table, three fingers of bourbon by his cup and saucer.

"What can I do you for, mister?" the

bartender said.

"Give my men what they want," Dryden said. "I'll have coffee."

When the men were served, Dryden said: "I'm looking for a man."

"Lot of them in town," the bartender said, his face closed.

"I'm not the law."

"Never said you was."

The bartender, a small, plump man with rosy cheeks and a kiss curl, polished a glass with a towel.

"A friend of mine, you understand," Dryden said. "I want to talk to him."

"Lot of men go in and out of here, friendly and otherwise," the bartender said. "I can't remember them all."

"His name is Clem Dredge, runs with a man named Simpson."

The bartender's face remained expressionless. "Neither one rings a bell with me."

Irritable now, Dryden said: "Then who the hell would know?"

"Well, you could try the other saloons. Eight of them in town."

"Do all the bartenders have the same bad memory as you?"

"I reckon."

"There's no one else who might know him?"

"Who?"

Pike saw Dryden fight back his anger. "Clem Dredge, damn it."

"Steve Morton might. He owns the sawmill and he's head of the local Vigilance Committee."

Dredge laid down his cup. "I'll go talk to him. Charlie, you come with me." He looked at the bartender. "I'll settle up when I get back."

"Settle up now, mister," the little man said. "I got the feeling you're not a good risk."

Steve Morton was a tall, wide-shouldered man with hard eyes. He wore a washed-out red vest with half-moons of sweat at the armpits.

Dryden had shaved that morning and with his trimmed imperial, silk top hat and frock coat he was an impressive figure.

Morton stood quietly, weighing Dryden, waiting for him to talk.

"Good morning," Dryden said.

Morton nodded.

"I wonder if you can help me."

"I'll try."

"I seem to have misplaced a friend of mine, a man named Clem Dredge."

Morton picked up a board and sighted

along the edge. "Never heard of him," he said.

"I was told he's here in Vamoose Gulch."

"Could be. But I still haven't heard of him."

Dryden produced a double eagle from his pocket. "Perhaps this will help you remember."

"You buying lumber, mister?"

"No."

"Then put your money away."

Dryden realized he was bucking a cold deck. "If you see Dredge, tell him I want to talk to him. I'll be at the Cactus Belle."

"I won't see him."

"But if you do . . ."

"Yeah, if I do, I'll tell him."

Morton looked at Pike's empty sleeve. "War?"

"No. Later."

"Too bad," Morton said.

Dryden was in a towering rage by the time he stepped into the saloon.

"You men," he said, "it's time you started earning your wages."

"What you want us to do?" McMullen said.

"Dredge is somewhere in town. Spread

266

out, find him. When you do, bring him back here."

The eleven gunmen exchanged glances, uncertain.

"Suppose he don't want to come?" a man asked.

"Suppose he don't want to come?" Dryden mimicked the man's high-pitched voice. "You're wearing a gun, aren't you? Make him come. If you're scared to go it alone, double up on him. But, damn your eyes, bring Dredge to me."

The gunmen shuffled out with all the enthusiasm of men walking to the gallows.

Dryden looked at Pike. "They drink my whiskey, eat my grub, but when it comes to doing what I hired them to do, they're a bunch of sniveling cowards."

Pike smiled. "Clem Dredge is a man to be reckoned with, Henry."

"And so am I," Dryden said.

Suddenly it dawned on Pike that Henry Dryden, not Clem Dredge, was the most dangerous man in Vamoose Gulch.

Chapter 42

Dryden's anger and frustration grew as one by one his men reported back to him. No one had seen Dredge. No one even knew who he was.

"When you mention Dredge's name in this town, it gets so quiet you could hear a worm sneeze," McMullen said.

"They'll protect one of their own, Henry," Pike said. "We're outsiders and maybe the law."

"He'll show," Dryden said. "We're pushing him and he won't like that."

"All he has to do is lie low until we leave," Pike said.

Dryden shook his head. "If he's in town, he'll show tonight. He may try to pick us off one at a time and that vigilante, Morton, won't try to stop him."

"Morton might even throw in with him," Pike said.

"There's a dozen of us. We can handle

Dredge and Morton."

"Eleven," Pike said. "Count me out."

He picked up his beer and took a seat on one of the rockers on the porch. Loretta was sitting in another.

Pike laid the beer at his feet and built a cigarette. "How was church?"

"I said a prayer for you, Charlie. And for my mother and for grandmother Sarah and for my sister who died when she was little. Then I said one for myself."

Pike lit his cigarette. "Did you say one for Henry?"

"No. The devil will look after his own."

Pike drank from the beer schooner. Loretta took it from him, had a swallow and handed it back.

"Henry's men don't go to church, huh?" she said.

"No, I guess they don't."

"If they had, they'd know where Clem Dredge and his boys are holed up."

Pike had been rocking; now he stopped and sat bolt upright. "They're in church?"

"Uh-huh. I guess Dredge figured it would be the last place Henry would think of looking for him."

"He didn't recognize you?"

"I don't think so. I sat at the back and Dredge and his boys were up front, passing a jug. They didn't even glance my way. I guess they're used to seeing whores at church in Vamoose Gulch."

"How many does he have with him?"

"Six. The only one I recognized was John Simpson."

Loretta looked at Pike. "You going to tell Henry?"

"Hell no."

"Why not?"

"Because if he doesn't meet up with Dredge, he won't need me and he'll let you go."

"My horse is right there at the rail, Charlie. I could make a break for it."

"He'd send men after you, Loretta. You can't take that chance."

"Then where the heck do we go from here, Charlie?"

"I have a feeling in my gut that a former outlaw by the name of Steve Morton is going to make that decision for us," Pike said.

The day shaded into night and lights blazed all over town. The saloons filled up, out-of-tune pianos jangled and rouged fancy ladies again plied their trade.

Pike and Loretta ate in one of the restaurants. Dryden, always careful, sent a glowering gunman along with them.

They returned to the saloon, but again preferred to sit outside, away from the smoke and noise.

It was there that Steve Morton and a dozen of his heavily armed vigilantes found them.

He spoke to Pike. "Is she with you?"

Pike nodded.

"Then both of you, inside."

Prodded by shotguns, Pike and Loretta stepped into the saloon.

The floor was thronged with men and laughing women, but it parted and fell silent when Morton and his men entered.

Dryden sat at a table, sharing a bottle and a blonde with McMullen, Cletus Tate and a couple of other men.

Morton walked directly to the table and leveled his sawn-off scattergun at Dryden's head.

"Call in your dogs, mister," he said. "All of them."

Dryden pushed the blonde off his lap and she fell with a bump onto the floor. "What is the meaning of this?" he said.

"The meaning is clear. You're leaving town." He motioned with the shotgun. "Now call in your dogs."

Dryden rose slowly to his feet, a dozen pairs of eyes watching his every move.

Morton's vigilantes were outlaws, killers, cold-eyed men who believed that their gun skills made them the law in Vamoose Gulch. Such men were not to be trifled with.

Dryden called to his boys and they drifted toward his table, a few of them already half drunk.

"Now we'll walk nice and peaceful to the livery," Morton said. "You'll saddle up and get out of town."

His eyes, cold and hard as iron, fixed on Pike. "That includes you, cowboy. The woman can stay."

Morton stared at Dryden. "And none of you ain't never coming back."

Dryden retreated into bluster. "This is an outrage. All I wanted to do was talk to an old friend. Damn it, you're treating me like a criminal."

"Maybe you haven't noticed, but we're all criminals in Vamoose Gulch, so you're being treated on the square," Morton said.

Shotguns in the hands of men who know how to use them make mighty persuasive arguments.

Dryden and his hard cases meekly rode out of town, the jeers of the crowd stinging them like thrown rocks.

Loretta had elected to ride with them.

"I can't leave you alone with Henry and

his bunch, Charlie," she'd said. "They'd eat you alive."

Dryden chose a campsite close to the town, well hidden in a dry wash concealed by wild oaks and brush.

He called a meeting immediately.

"Men, we are too few to invest the town, but I want the trails in and out watched constantly," he said. "When Dredge tries to leave, we'll get him."

Dragged away from whores and whiskey, the gunmen were surly.

And the prospect of playing watchmen under a blazing-hot sun did nothing to improve their mood.

Sensing their discontent, Dryden threw them a bone.

"Before we leave, we'll torch the town, burn it down around their ears." In a dramatic gesture, he threw out his arms, his voice rising. "What do you say, boys? Will we teach those outlaws that they can't humiliate Henry Dryden's boys and get away with it?"

If the judge expected a cheer, he didn't get it.

His words were met with empty eyes and a sullen silence.

Dryden's threat to burn the town was real

enough. Its tinder-dry buildings were terribly vulnerable to flame and would go up like firecrackers.

"One thing more, men," he said, ignoring his defeat. "If you see a Chinaman on a mule, bring him to me."

Now there was a stir of interest.

"Where the hell is he coming from — China?" a man said.

"No," Dryden said, "from the direction of Eagle Pass. Don't let him enter Vamoose Gulch, bring him here."

"What's he look like?" McMullen asked.

"Hell, like a Chinaman," Dryden said. "Even you will recognize a Chinaman, Mr. McMullen."

This time the judge was rewarded by grudging laughter.

"I'll set the watches at sunup," Dryden said. "You men get your coffee and then grab some sleep."

Dryden sat beside Pike and Loretta and lit a cigar.

"What did I do to deserve such idiots?" he said.

"Maybe you should go to church more often, Henry," Pike said.

CHAPTER 43

Three days later, while Dredge was still holed up in Vamoose Gulch, a grinning Mc-Mullen brought in the Chinaman and his flea-bitten mule.

Dryden was effusive.

"Chang, so good to see you again," he said, returning the tiny man's deep bow. "How was New Orleans?"

"Very busy, Judge," Chang said. "Big gang wars, many die. Much business for Chang."

The Chinese was a small, wizened man with mild brown eyes. He wore traditional robes and a long pigtail that hung from a round, silk hat. His teeth were small and black.

When Dryden introduced Chang to Pike, the little man bowed and said: "Judge good man. Hang many bandits."

"With your help on occasion, Mr. Chang," Dryden said.

"I helped when I could," Chang said,

beaming.

Later, as Chang sat by the fire boiling a handful of rice, Dryden took Pike aside.

"The Chinaman is the second-to-last piece of the puzzle, Charlie," he said. "Now all we need is Dryden."

"What is the answer to the puzzle, Henry?"

"You will learn that in due course. Let me just say that Mr. Chang is the key."

"The Celestial doesn't look like he could torture anybody," Pike said.

"Appearances are deceptive, Charlie. He is very good at making a tough man talk."

"How the hell did he get to this country?"

"Chang had to flee his native land after he ran afoul of the dowager empress for some reason," Dryden said. "He's a eunuch, you know."

"What's that?"

"When he was young, they cut off his balls."

"That could give a man an attitude, I guess."

Dryden shrugged. "Eunuchs are highly regarded in China. He was probably a scribe of some kind and part-time court torturer. Mr. Chang doesn't talk much about his past."

"Any one of your gun trash could get

Dredge to talk," Pike said.

"I tried that once before and it didn't work," Dryden said.

"You mean the dead man who rode into my ranch?"

"He did? How harrowing for you, Charlie."

"He was a . . . whatever that word is. You made him that way."

"He was spying on you, Charlie. We were protecting your interests."

"But he wouldn't tell you where Dredge was?"

"He might have, but the ham-handed fools I have around me killed him."

"Chang doesn't kill people?"

"He might, eventually. But he keeps them alive for a very long time."

Pike shook his head. "Dryden, how did you ever get to be a judge?"

"Because my strong right hand struck down the scum of the frontier. I hanged the thieves, the robbers, the murderers, the good-for-nothings who lived by deceit and treachery."

Dryden smiled. "Like Mr. Chang I was good at my task. And that, Charlie, is why I was a judge."

"You ever consider that you deserve to hang as much as the men you killed?"

"No, I never consider that."

"You should."

"The law doesn't apply to men like me, who served it well and loyally."

"Nobody is above the law, Henry."

Dryden put his hand on Pike's shoulder. "It doesn't matter anyway. Soon I'll be too rich to hang." He winked. "And so will you, Charlie."

Pike felt his skin under Dryden's hand begin to crawl.

"He doesn't mention dying anymore," Loretta said.

"Soon he'll be too rich to die," Pike said.

"Is that what he thinks?"

"I reckon so."

Loretta picked up her steaming coffee cup by the rim. She looked across at the fire. "That Chinaman scares me, Charlie."

"He should."

"Why is he here?"

"Dryden will use him to convince Dredge."

"Of what?"

"That it might be a good idea to reveal where he hid his gold."

Loretta smiled as she laid down her cup. "That little man is going to scare Clem Dredge, huh?"

"I think he will. Unless Dredge kills him first."

"What about us, Charlie?"

"Us?"

"Yeah, will we still be aboveground when all this is over?"

"I don't know, Loretta."

"That's not very reassuring."

"No, it's not."

Loretta stared into the darkness. "Henry hasn't come near me, you know. Not with a whip or the thing between his legs."

"He knows I'd kill him if he did. Or die trying."

"Charlie, how brave. You should be in a Walter Scott novel."

"More likely a dime novel: 'Charlie Pike Versus the Hanging Judge.' "

"It's got a ring to it," Loretta said. "But I think I like you better as a gallant knight."

"Well, I —"

Pike never completed what he had to say. A man rode into camp on a lathered horse and yelled: "He's leaving town!"

Dryden sprang to his feet. "Is it Dredge? Are you sure?"

"It's him all right, Judge. Seen him plain in the moonlight, heading north. Him an' five others."

"Mount up, men!" Dryden yelled. "This time we've got him, by God!"

CHAPTER 44

Dryden sent a rider to the south of town to bring in the men.

He grinned as he led his saddled horse past Pike. "He's ours, Charlie. We have him dead to rights."

"Henry, Dredge has already whittled down your numbers," Pike said, "and he's got J. M. Simpson and Mexican Bob with him."

"What are you saying, Charlie?"

"That you need more men."

Dryden stopped. "I won't fight him on his ground, Charlie. We will hit him hard when he least expects it."

"Dredge is an outlaw. He rides wary and sleeps with one eye open."

"Let me worry about that."

Dryden swung into the saddle. "Loretta will ride with the main column. You will scout Dredge's line of march. If he turns back or swings east for Texas, you will let me know."

"Where will you be, Henry?"

"To the rear of Dredge's column. But first I have some unfinished business to attend to in Vamoose Gulch."

"There are women and children in the town."

"That is not my problem. When I am mistreated, I will not let the transgression go unpunished."

"The vigilantes will come after you, Henry," Pike said. "Depend on it."

"I doubt it. They'll be too busy trying to save their miserable burg."

"You'll be caught between Dredge and a posse of hardcase outlaws. And like you, they don't forgive and forget easily."

Dryden smiled, a cold grimace. "Life is all about taking chances, Charlie."

He kneed his horse into motion. "Now mount up and you too, Loretta. It's time for Henry Dryden to make some mischief."

Pike tried. As soon as Dryden and his men pulled out, he rode a mile north, then swung back, heading for Vamoose Gulch.

A few minutes' warning was better than no warning at all.

But even by moonlight, a man doesn't ride a galloping horse across rough and broken country. Pike was forced to slow to a trot, his eyes searching the way ahead.

He was too late.

Vamoose Gulch, a dry powder keg, was already burning.

Pike drew rein.

In the distance men were yelling and shots rang out, shattering the night. People were already streaming out of town, clutching what few possessions they could carry.

As far as Pike could tell, the fire had started at the livery stable and had rapidly spread from there. The smell of burning timber carried in the wind and with it tiny flakes of white ash.

Dryden and his riders burst from the north end of town.

Close by, but hidden by darkness, Pike's eyes scanned the scarlet-tinged darkness. He spotted one riderless horse, then another.

It seemed as though Dryden's mad vengeance had cost him another two men.

The odds were slowly tilting in Clem Dredge's favor.

People, mostly women and children, were still evacuating the town. But as yet there was no sign of pursuit. Most of the horses would be in the livery stable and men would be trying to save those that hadn't already died.

Horses, maddened by fire, are unmanageable. It would be a long while before Vamoose Gulch, or what was left of it, could mount a posse.

Pike let his head sink to his chest, a sense of bitter defeat in him.

He had tried and failed to warn the town. Now what was left to him?

Loretta was still with Dryden, a hostage to his good behavior. If he simply rode away now, she would die. And Dryden's way of killing her would be terrible and full of pain.

He didn't love the woman, didn't even particularly like her. But he couldn't leave Loretta to her fate. Not if he still wanted to call himself a man.

Wearily, Pike swung his horse north. He felt as though an anvil were sitting on his shoulders.

The sky behind him was dull crimson, pillared by columns of black smoke, like the entrance hall to hell.

CHAPTER 45

Pike rode through the night, passing Dryden and his gunmen in the darkness.

At first light, he spotted Dredge's dust in the distance and rode close enough to see him and his men swing into Texas where Las Moras Creek met the Rio Bravo.

Dredge was riding into rolling prairie country, shaggy with tall grass, banded by forests of juniper and wild oak.

Keeping to the cover of the trees, Pike followed the outlaws for two miles.

Dredge stayed close to the south bank of the creek, heading northwest. The only town of any size in that direction was Brackettville, a stage stop on the old San Antonio–El Paso Road and a supply depot for the Tenth Cavalry at nearby Fort Clark.

By instinct and inclination, Clem Dredge was a city animal and it looked to Pike that he planned on going to ground in the town.

Swinging the dun around, Pike recrossed

the river, then waited, using his glass to scout for Dryden and his riders.

The judge showed up just before noon, nine men behind him, one of them bent over in the saddle, coughing up black blood.

Loretta took up the rear, her parasol shading her from a pitiless sun.

Pike told Dryden what he'd seen.

"Damn the man, damn his eyes," Dryden said.

Sweat beaded his forehead and he was working himself into a rage.

"He's forced me into another damned town."

Pike smiled. "I would suggest that you don't try to burn this one, Henry."

"Charlie, one day that impertinent tongue of yours will get you in trouble," Dryden snapped.

Dave McMullen rode beside Dryden. "Judge, Luke needs a doctor real bad."

"Not much a doctor can do for a gut-shot man," Dryden said.

He looked at Pike. "How far is this Brackettville place?"

"We can be there by nightfall," Pike said.

"Mr. McMullen, will the wounded man last that long?" Dryden said.

"No telling with a belly wound," McMullen said.

"He's slowing us down and we must be pressing on," Dryden said. "We'll make him as comfortable as we can and leave him here."

"A man shouldn't die alone," McMullen said. "And the rest of the men won't like it."

"I don't give a damn what the men like or don't like," Dryden said. "We're leaving him here."

"Judge, don't leave me to die like a dog," the man called Luke said. He was very young, with the soft face of a boy. He wore two guns, the mark of the wannabe bad man. "I need a doctor."

"Too late for doctors," Dryden said. "You're gut shot and you won't last until dark. I'm sorry, but we must ride on."

"Henry, I'll stay with him," Loretta said.

"No, you won't. I need you close."

Dryden turned to Pike. "Charlie, put him in shade somewhere. We'll take his horse but leave him his guns."

Then, in a rare act of compassion, Dryden took a pint of whiskey from his saddlebags. "Give him this. It will help ease the pain."

Argument was useless and Pike accepted that fact.

He dismounted and led the boy's horse to a grove of wild oak. Luke bit back a scream as Pike helped him from his saddle and into shade.

"You won't leave me here," the kid said.

Pike opened Luke's shirt. He'd taken the bullet an inch under his navel and there was no recovering from a wound like that.

Despite all that had happened to him, Pike had not lost the habit of kindness. But he was sore put to bring the boy any measure of comfort.

He said what had to be said, hating himself for saying it.

"Luke, there might be animals around. If there are, go to your guns. Later, when you feel it's time, drink the whiskey and use the last round on yourself."

The boy's blue eyes were clouded with hurt.

"That's hard, mister," he said. "Mighty hard and cold."

"You got tough times coming down, boy," Pike said.

"Then leave me, damn you. Let me die in peace."

Pike watched as Dryden and his men rode out. None spared a glance for the dying boy, not wishing to see a small, human tragedy they could not change.

"I'm sorry, Luke," Pike said. He placed the flat of his hand on the boy's chest. "Ride easy, pard."

He rose to his feet and stepped to his horse. Then froze as a gunshot racketed.

Luke — Pike never did learn the boy's last name — had killed himself.

"I sure don't blame you none, boy," Pike said. "And neither will the good Lord, I reckon."

He picked up the pint of whiskey and drank deep.

"I heard a shot," Dryden said. "Did you put him out of his misery?"

"No, Henry, he did that his own self."

Loretta's eyes misted. "He was only a boy."

"There," Dryden said, "speaks a whore with a heart of gold."

"Well, Henry, where do you go from here?" Pike said.

"We will ride into Brackettville, or whatever the burg is called, stay together and see what develops."

"Not much of a plan, Henry."

"Do you have a better one?"

"Can't say as I do."

"Then mine will suffice."

Pike turned in the saddle, then said: "Where's the Chinaman?"

"He'll be along. Chang sets his own pace."

"You start a shooting war in Brackettville and you could end up writing your name on the wall of the local calaboose," Pike said. "It's a tough town."

"I don't recall saying anything about shooting," Dryden said.

"Then what?"

"I said we'd see what develops."

"Henry," Pike said, "you're riding into big trouble."

"We'll soon find out, Charlie, won't we?"

CHAPTER 46

Despite a recent flood, Brackettville was in the middle of a prosperity boom when Pike and the others rode in. Soldiers and civilians from Fort Clark thronged the streets, and the mercantiles and saloons were ablaze with light, doing a thriving business.

As he'd done in Vamoose Gulch, Dryden set up his headquarters in a saloon, but this time he ordered the horses be kept at the hitching rail.

He had ordered Loretta to join him at the bar. "And you too, Charlie," he'd said.

Dryden's sullen gunmen found women and whiskey and dispersed into the crowd. But Dave McMullen, the fastest gun among them, stayed close.

After Pike ordered a rye and a beer, Dryden waited until he built a smoke, then said: "I have a plan, Charlie."

"Does it involve me?"

"Yes, very much so."

"Then count me out, Henry."

"You'll merely be an observer, Charlie," Dryden said. "Mr. McMullen and Loretta will do the heavy lifting."

"What's on your mind?" Pike said.

Dryden looked around him, making sure there was no one within earshot.

"Loretta, get yourself a hotel room and make yourself pretty. Not whore pretty, respectable lady pretty."

He gave her a double eagle. "If you don't have what you need, buy it."

Loretta was suspicious. "What the heck are you up to, Henry?"

"I plan to use you as bait, my dear. You will draw the moth to my flame."

"Loretta's not catching your drift, Henry, and neither am I," Pike said.

"It's simple. We're pretty certain that Clem Dredge is in town, are we not?"

"I'd say that's a good guess," Pike said.

"Good. Then Loretta will go from saloon to saloon, a respectable, weepy, young virgin from Boston town in search of her long-lost brother."

"Nobody's going to buy me as a virgin, Henry," Loretta said.

Dryden smiled. "I know it's a stretch, dear, but do your best. The only person you have to convince is Clem Dredge."

"Dredge!"

"Yes. Using your . . . ah . . . feminine wiles, lure him out of whatever hellhole he's in by inviting him home with you. Invent whatever lie you need, but get him out of there."

"Suppose he doesn't want to come?" Loretta said.

"My dear, Dredge is an animal," Dryden said. "He won't pass on the chance to bust an innocent young virgin wide open."

"I don't have a home, Henry," Loretta said.

"I know, but it doesn't matter. Once Dredge is outside, in an alley preferably, Mr. McMullen will take him down."

"You mean shoot the son of a bitch?" McMullen asked.

"No, you idiot," Dryden said. "I want him alive. Knock him over the head with a club or something."

"And then?" McMullen asked.

"Then we smuggle Dredge out of town and leave him to the tender mercies of Mr. Chang."

"Where do I fit in all this?" Pike asked.

"You will accompany Loretta and Mr. McMullen."

"Why?"

"To see that Loretta does not attract the

unwelcome attention of other men besides Dredge."

"Send one of your other boys, Henry."

"No, I want you to go, Charlie. You're handy with a gun and good with your fists." Dryden smiled. "Or should I say fist?"

He ordered another drink, then said: "You're the ideal man to go, Charlie. No one, including Dredge, will feel threatened by a one-armed man."

"He might recognize me, Henry. Have you thought of that?"

"No, I had not. Will he?"

"I don't know."

"Then that's a chance we'll have to take." After a few moments' thought, he said: "More to the point, will you be able to recognize Dredge?"

"I only saw him at a distance, but I'll remember him," Pike said.

Dryden grabbed Loretta's arm roughly. "You understand what I told you? How to dress and act?"

"Suppose I don't want to do it?" Loretta said.

"Then I'll kill you, my dear," Dryden said. "You have a simple choice to make."

"It's you who's the animal, Henry," Loretta said.

"Perhaps. Now, will you do as I say?"

"You left me with no other option."

"Yes, I did, didn't I?"

Dryden turned to McMullen. "Go with her. When she's ready, come back here and get Charlie."

After Loretta and the gunman left, Dryden said: "When Mr. McMullen accomplishes his task, come and tell me, Charlie."

"This isn't going to work," Pike said. "Too many ifs, buts and maybes."

"Once again, do you have a better plan?"

"No."

"Then it has to work. It will be much better for you if it does, Charlie. I assure you of that."

CHAPTER 47

Loretta and McMullen returned to the saloon two hours later.

Brackettville was just getting into full swing and booted and belted men crowded the bar and tables, raucous and flushed by whiskey.

"My, my, my, you've transformed yourself, Loretta," Dryden said above the din. "The perfect little lady."

Pike had to agree with him.

Loretta wore a demure dress of gray silk, her bustle was only as large as it had to be and a straw boater perched on top of her upswept curls.

She looked very pretty and as shy and modest as a big city schoolmarm.

But when she opened her mouth, it was obvious that here was a gal who had been up the creek and over the mountains.

"This damn pervert watched my every move," she said, waving a hand at the grinning McMullen. "He can tell you what color of bloomers I'm wearing."

"I can tell you the color of more than that," McMullen said.

"Damn pervert!"

Dryden put a finger to his lips. "Careful of your language, Loretta," he said. "Remember, you're supposed to be a lady."

He looked around the saloon. "Let's give it a trial. Mingle, start looking for your dear brother."

"Here?"

"Yes, here. Obviously you need practice if you hope to convince Clem Dredge."

Later Pike would admit to himself that Loretta pulled it off well.

A hard-as-nails whore, with a wellspring of knowledge of every sin a man could commit, plus a few she'd invented herself, she was suddenly as innocent and wide eyed as her Walter Scott heroine.

Loretta moved among rough men, punchers, soldiers, miners, gamblers, loungers and frontier toughs, telling them she was undone, heartbroken, ready to faint at any moment.

"Have you seen him?" she pleaded. "A young man of good family who may have fallen in with low companions."

Western men walked a fine line when it

came to respectable women.

In some towns, mistreatment of such women would be tolerated if apologies were made and the miscreant vowed to never again cross the deadline into the picket fence neighborhood. In others, abuse of a decent woman could get a man hanged. Brackettville was one of those.

Loretta was given a polite hearing. She gave a vague description of her missing brother and sympathetic men made earnest promises to "be on the scout for him."

After her performance, Dryden hustled Loretta outside. Pike and McMullen joined him.

"You did very well, my dear," Dryden said. "Now repeat that in every saloon in town until we find Dredge."

"Suppose he isn't even here, Henry?" Loretta said.

"Then we've been wasting our time, haven't we?"

Dryden looked at McMullen. "You know what to do. Charlie will point Dredge out to you. Don't fail me, Mr. McMullen."

"If he's in town, I'll get him," the gunman said.

"Good, now all three of you be on your way and good luck."

■ ■ ■ ■

They tried the Bon-Ton, the Silver Nugget, the Bucket of Blood, O'Hara's Taproom, the Main Chance and half a dozen others.

Loretta was becoming bored and irritable and her acting performance was suffering.

The hour was growing late and the crowds were thinning.

"Dredge isn't here," Loretta said. "We're wasting our time."

"Once more, Loretta. Then we'll call it quits," Pike said.

"Along the street there at the edge of town," McMullen said. "The Last Chance."

"Well, that's really appropriate," Loretta said, "because then I'm done. My feet are killing me and I need a drink."

"Looks like a dive," Pike said.

"Then if Clem Dredge is in town, that's where he'll be."

"I can't go in there," Pike said.

"Why the hell not?" McMullen said.

"The saloons aren't crowded any longer and Dredge has a couple of men who might recognize me. We can't take the chance."

"Hell, man, just walk in, identify Dredge, then skip out again."

"I figured I could do that in a crowded

saloon and get away with it," Pike said. "But there's only two horses at the hitching rail."

"So?" McMullen said.

"So, if he's here, Dredge will be staying in town, you idiot," Loretta said. "His horses will be in the livery. That means only his boys and a couple of other men will be in the saloon."

"All right, Pike, describe him to me," Mc-Mullen said.

"No, you stay outside and lay for Dredge if he's in there," Loretta said.

"What's he look like, Charlie?"

"Big, bearded man, looks like a bear. He'll be with a mean-looking Mexican and a towhead who goes by the name of Buff Kelly."

"That should be easy enough," Loretta said.

"If he's inside, get him out here, Loretta," Pike said. "Say you'll take him back to your hotel room and show him a tintype of your brother. Say anything, just get him away from the saloon."

"Waste of time, but I'll try it," Loretta said.

CHAPTER 48

The Last Chance lay beyond a three-story grain-and-feed warehouse. Between was a patch of open ground with a substantial corral. In front, half a dozen freight wagons were parked alongside a heavy army dray.

Darkness pooled like gloomy lakes at the rear of the warehouse and saloon and the moon cast down the posts and boards of the corral and spilled them across the ground, an elongated grid of pearl white and gray.

Pike watched Loretta lift her skirts and step onto the stretch of boardwalk in front of the saloon; then he and McMullen moved behind the dray.

McMullen drew his Colt and touched his tongue to his top lip.

Pike knew McMullen wasn't scared, but, like himself, the gunman was sensing the night. The darkness seemed full of menace and the air was as cold as stone.

Minutes ticked past . . . and irritation flared in Pike.

What the hell was Loretta doing in there?

Suddenly there was movement in the street. McMullen, with the honed reaction of the revolver fighter, was instantly alert, his eyes scanning the gloom.

A drunk staggered toward them, a bottle in his hand, a fractured version of "Lorena" on his lips, sung at the top of his lungs.

McMullen swore.

"Get back into the shadows," Pike whispered.

The drunk lurched closer.

The man stopped at the open ground, took a swig from his bottle and studied the wagons, blinking. He stepped closer.

Carefully, he laid his bottle on a wagon seat. Then he opened his pants and hosed a tremendous, arching stream of piss into the darkness.

Pike heard McMullen's sharp intake of breath as piss rattled around him.

"Son of a bitch," the gunman muttered.

"Huh?" the drunk said. "Is anybody there?"

The man stared like an owl for a few moments, then shrugged and picked up his bottle.

He wandered away, back the way he'd come.

"Pissed all over my boots," McMullen said after the drunk was out of earshot.

He kicked moisture off his toes. "Son of a bitch! If I knew for sure that Dredge wasn't in the saloon, I'd go put a bullet into him."

"Nice song, though," Pike said.

"What?"

" 'Lorena,' the song he was singing. It was real nice."

"Pike," McMullen said, "you go to hell."

The saloon door burst open.

Clem Dredge, huge and bearded, walked outside, his arm around Loretta's waist. Behind him stepped Mexican Bob and five others.

"Don't you worry none, little girlie," Dredge was saying. "You leave it to me. We'll go back to the hotel, get to know each other better an' then we'll go look for your poor, lost brother."

As he walked past Pike's hiding place, his gunmen around him, Dredge said: "Fell in with bad company, you say?"

"Oh yes, sir," Loretta said in a small voice, still playing her role to the hilt. "I'm so worried. I fear I am quite undone."

"Hell, that's not all that's gonna be undone," a man said.

Dredge turned. "Kelly, you shut your trap." Then to Loretta: "You're safe with me, little Boston lady darlin'. Uncle Clem will take care of you real good."

His hand on Loretta's ass, Dredge and his men faded into the darkness. "Why, I mind the time . . ." Pike heard Dredge say, but his voice too dwindled and died away.

"Now what do we do?" McMullen said. "I can't get near the son of a bitch."

"We go after him," Pike said.

"At the hotel?"

"Yeah. He'll want to be alone with Loretta in her room. We can get to him there."

"Thin, Pike."

"Got a better idea, like telling Dryden we failed him?"

McMullen had no answer for that question.

The Crown Hotel was a two-story, timber building with a picket fence and a porch in front.

Pike and McMullen stepped into the foyer and crossed to the clerk's desk.

"I need the number of my sister's room," Pike said.

"Her name?" the clerk said. He was a small man with pomaded black hair and a prim mouth.

Pike felt a moment of panic. What the hell was Loretta calling herself?

"She's a small, blond girl," he said. "She just walked in a few minutes ago with her intended . . . ah . . . husband."

"I'm sorry, sir," the clerk said, "but I can't give out a room number without a name."

"Loretta," Pike said.

The clerk shook his head and his mouth puckered. "There is no lady by that name in the hotel."

McMullen's gun came up fast. He shoved the muzzle between the clerk's eyes and thumbed back the hammer.

"She's with a man called Clem Dredge and five other hard cases," he said. The gun pressed harder into the bridge of the clerk's nose. "Now do you remember?"

"Room twenty-four," the clerk said, his throat bobbing. "Just turn right at the top of the stairs."

"I'm obliged," McMullen said.

"Dave, you can be mighty persuasive when you try," Pike said as they climbed the stairs.

"Trouble with you, Pike, is that you try too hard to be nice. I ain't nice."

Every step the two men took on the uncarpeted hallway made the floor timbers creak.

Pike swallowed hard.

If Dredge's gunmen heard them and came out to investigate, it would mean a close-range revolver fight. And there would be no victors, only dead men.

Room 24 was at the end of the hall. As Pike and McMullen stepped closer, noisy as men walking on gravel, the door swung open.

Pike's gun was up and ready.

CHAPTER 49

Loretta stood in the doorway. Her dress had been ripped off her left shoulder and an unruly strand of hair fell over her forehead. She beckoned the two men inside, then closed the door behind them.

"I'm sure you two idiots could have made more noise if you'd tried real hard," she said.

Pike didn't answer. All his attention was on Dredge, sprawled facedown on the floor, the back of his head bloody.

"You didn't kill him, did you?" Pike said.

"I don't know," Loretta said. "Damn pervert."

She pointed to a bruise that marred the ivory swell of her right breast. "Look, he bit me on the tit, hard."

Pike kneeled beside Dredge. The man was still breathing.

He looked at Loretta. "What the hell did you hit him with?"

"That." She pointed to a heavy iron poker lying on the floor.

"Damn, you sure put out his fire," Pike said.

"Serves him right, damn degenerate," Loretta said.

"You sure you're in the right business?" Pike said.

"What do we do now?" McMullen asked.

"Get him outside."

"How the hell we gonna do that? Drag him along the hall? His boys will hear us for sure."

"We'll find another way."

Pike stepped to the window, threw it open and looked outside.

A narrow, bottle-strewn alley lay between the hotel and the restaurant next door. He looked down into the gloom and calculated the drop from the window to the alley was about twenty feet.

Behind him Dredge groaned.

"He's coming to," Loretta said. "Want me to hit him again?"

"No, but we need to get him out of here now, before he wakes up," Pike said.

"How?" McMullen said.

"We'll throw him out the window."

"Hell, man, you'll kill him."

"Feetfirst. It's a chance we'll have to take."

"We'll break his damned neck," Mc-Mullen said.

"I've only got one arm," Pike said. "I can't manhandle a man his size along the hall and down the stairs. And the clerk would surely call the law."

He grabbed Dredge by one booted ankle. "Now help me. You too, Loretta."

Between them they got Dredge to the window. The man was groaning and his eyes fluttered.

"Now!" Pike said.

Dredge hit the ground with a thud and a clank of bottles.

"Is he still alive?" McMullen asked.

"I hope so," Pike said.

"He's lying there very quiet," Loretta said.

"He just fell twenty feet," Pike said. "Of course he's quiet."

He shut the window, then said: "Right, one at a time along the hallway. And be as quiet as you can. Loretta, ladies first."

"We're all going to die," Loretta said.

"Get Dryden over here and the rest of the men," Pike told McMullen.

They were crowded around Dredge's crumpled shape. The outlaw was still groaning. His eyes were rolling in his head and there were flecks of spittle on his lips.

"We killed the son of a bitch," McMullen said.

"Go," Pike said, "get Dryden."

The moon was sliding lower in the sky and the wind gusted into the alley, lifting pieces of paper that fluttered in the air like stricken birds.

There was no one on the street. Somewhere a dog barked, a man shouted and the dog yelped into silence.

Dryden, McMullen beside him, stepped into the alley. Behind him his men stood with the horses.

"Did you kill him?" Dryden said, his face worried.

"No, he's alive all right," Pike said.

"Let's get him on a horse," Dryden said.

"He doesn't have a horse," McMullen said.

"I know that, Mr. McMullen. Hog-tie him and put him across the back of your horse. Quickly now."

Dryden turned. "A couple of you men, lend a hand here."

They walked their horses out of Brackettville without attracting the attention of late-night revelers or a patrolling lawman.

Dryden led the way southwest, heading back along Las Moras Creek.

There was still enough moonlight to light the trail, though the land and trees around them were lost in darkness. The wind played among the juniper and live oaks, a constant rustling heard but not seen.

Pike rode beside Dryden. He was uneasy and constantly checked their back trail.

"I don't expect pursuit, Charlie," Dryden said.

"I do. Dredge's boys will come after us."

"They won't discover he's gone until morning. By then we'll be across the Rio Bravo."

"They'll follow us into Mexico."

"Of course they will and we'll be ready for them."

As dawn was breaking, they crossed the river and headed due west in the direction of the Madres.

At noon, as the heat of the day became intense, Dryden ordered camp to be made in a small meadow between two oak-covered hills.

There was a running stream, a few cotton-woods growing on its banks and a draw where they could put up the horses.

Dryden ordered a pair of riflemen to the hilltops to keep watch.

"We'll wait here for the Chinaman," he

311

said to Pike.

"How will he know where to find us?"

"The Chinaman will find us. I don't understand how he does it, some kind of strange, heathen instinct, I suppose."

He worked a kink out of his back, then said: "Well, Charlie, shall we go check on Dredge?" Dryden smiled. "He is our meal ticket, after all."

CHAPTER 50

Clem Dredge was conscious and black with rage.

"Get these ropes off me, Dryden," he said.

"Ah, Mr. Dredge, I'm so glad you suffered no permanent harm from your unfortunate defenestration."

"What the hell are you talking about?" Dredge said.

"I guess he means when I threw you out the window," Pike said.

"You did that?"

"Guilty."

Dredge struggled with his bonds, teeth bared. "I'll kill you. I swear to God I'll rip your heart out and stomp on it."

"Charlie, I'm afraid you've upset Mr. Dredge," Dryden said.

The outlaw scowled. "Are you Charlie Pike, the son of a bitch with the ranch in the Brazos country?"

"Guilty again. And I'm the one who put a

bullet into you at San Fermin."

"It was you, up there in the rocks?" Dredge said.

"Yeah, me. You cost me an arm, Dredge, and just winging a piece of shit like you wasn't worth it."

"I did it, damn you," Dredge said. He grinned and his teeth looked as if they were covered in green algae. "Saw my bullet hit, saw your damned arm explode."

Dredge turned his attention back to Dryden. "Untie these ropes, you."

"Not now, maybe later. Or maybe not."

"If I ever get loose, I'll kill you, Dryden. I'll kill you twice over, once for my brother and once for the sheer fun of it."

"Mr. Dredge, currently I'd say you're not in a position to make threats to anybody," Dryden said.

"Damn you, what do you want from me?" Dredge said.

"An answer."

"What answer?"

"The answer to a question you will be asked very soon."

"You're not in court any longer, Dryden. I don't have to answer any of your questions."

"I suspected that would be your attitude, Mr. Dredge. And that is why a gentleman of my acquaintance will be your interrogator."

"What the hell are you saying, Dryden?"

"Soon you will meet a man, a Celestial, and he will put a question to you. How you answer will determine whether you live or die."

"Are you talking about a damned Chinaman?"

"Indeed. His name is Mr. Chang."

Pike guessed that Dredge had heard the name, sometime, somewhere. It showed in the man's eyes, as though deep in the dark canyons of his reptilian mind he felt a vague fear.

"What's the question, Dryden?"

"I will let Mr. Chang ask it," Dryden said.

"I ain't telling a damned Chinaman nothing," Dredge said.

"Oh, but you will, Mr. Dredge." Dryden smiled. "Believe me, you will."

Dryden turned and walked away.

"You, Pike, what's the question?" Dredge asked,

"I don't know," Pike said. "But for your sake, I hope you have the answer."

Charlie Pike saw the trouble start from way off.

Drowsy, his back against a tree, he idly

watched McMullen and another man climb the hills to relieve the watch.

But McMullen's man didn't immediately come down, as a sentry with a coffee thirst or a desire for sleep would.

Instead he and McMullen talked for some time, then both descended the hill together.

Pike moved his head and his eyes went to the other hill. The same thing was happening; two men were coming down.

It could mean nothing. But Pike sensed something brewing that spelled trouble for Dryden.

It wasn't long in coming.

Dryden was sleeping in the shade, a forearm over his eyes.

McMullen stood at his feet and said: "Get up, Judge. We got talking to do."

The rest of the men were in an arc behind him, all of them carrying rifles.

Dryden woke instantly, his hand instinctively reaching for his gun.

McMullen had been carrying his Winchester over his shoulder. Now it slapped into his left palm and leveled.

"Money talk, Judge," McMullen said. "We don't want gun talk."

Dryden rose to his feet. A distance away, Dredge watched him intently, an amused smile on his lips.

"What can I do for you, Mr. McMullen?" Dryden asked.

"We're pulling out, Judge. Time to pay us our due."

"But your task is not yet complete."

"We signed on to find you Clem Dredge. Well, we found him."

"But what about his men? No doubt they're on the way."

"That's your fight, Judge, not ours."

McMullen turned his head. "What do you say, boys?"

"Damn right," a man said, and the rest murmured their agreement.

"And share the wages of our dead among us," McMullen said.

"What if I don't?"

"Then I'll drop you right where you stand."

McMullen stared at Pike. "Charlie Pike, you taking cards in this game?"

"Not my fight either, Dave," Pike said.

Loretta, propped against a tree behind Dryden, suddenly realized she was in the line of fire. She rose and sat beside Pike. "Fun time we're having, huh?"

Pike smiled but made no answer.

Dryden's mouth was a tight, white line, his entire body tense.

"Don't even consider it, Judge," Mc-

Mullen said. "You wouldn't clear leather."

"One of you, get his gun," he said.

A man lifted Dryden's gun from his shoulder holster. "In his vest pocket," McMullen said. "He carries a hideout."

After he was relieved of his derringer, Dryden's face was murderous.

"I should have known better than put my trust in vile scum like you, McMullen," he said.

"We live and learn, Judge," McMullen said. His face hardened. "Where's your poke?"

Dryden said nothing.

"I'll gun you in one second, Judge. Where's your poke?"

"My strongbox is in my saddlebags, damn you."

"Get it, Kyle," McMullen said to one of his men.

"I won't forget this, McMullen," Dryden said. "I won't rest until I see you hang."

McMullen smiled. "Hang me? How the hell you plan on doing that? You ain't a judge no more."

"Believe me, I'll find a way."

"Yeah, when pigs fly."

The man called Kyle walked up to McMullen, hefting the box in both hands, bending backward against the weight.

"Heavy poke, Dave."

He dropped his clinking burden at McMullen's feet.

"How much you reckon?" McMullen said.

"I don't know. A lot."

"Damn you, McMullen, all that money is not yours," Dryden said. "It represents the savings of a lifetime."

McMullen ignored him. "Kyle, the rest of you, saddle the horses," he said. "We're getting out of here."

"And now you're a common thief, McMullen," Dryden said.

"Seems like, Judge."

McMullen tied the box to his saddle horn and mounted. "Loretta," he said, "you want to come with us?"

"I'll stick," Loretta said.

McMullen nodded and touched his hat to Dryden. "Thanks for everything, Judge."

"I'll see you in hell," Dryden said, trembling with rage.

McMullen smiled and swung his horse away.

A split second later his lower jaw was blown clean off.

CHAPTER 51

Dave McMullen swayed in the saddle, his face a grotesque mask of blood and bone. A second bullet lifted dust from his shirtfront and he toppled to the ground.

Pike was on his feet, gun in hand.

Dredge's men, if that's who they were, had positioned themselves on top of both hills and fired steadily into the meadow.

Three saddles had emptied and McMullen's horse was galloping away wildly, its reins trailing.

The half dozen surviving gunmen were professionals and they'd been in scrapes like this before. They dismounted and took whatever cover they could find, returning fire.

Dredge roared with laughter.

"Damn you, Dryden," he yelled, "you'll eat supper in hell."

A bullet kicked up dust near Loretta.

Pike grabbed her arm and shoved her into

the oaks.

"Stay down," he said.

"Are they Dredge's men?" she asked, her eyes frightened.

"That would be my guess," Pike said.

He ducked as a shot rattled through the tree branches, then another.

At first Dryden seemed stunned. But then he gathered himself, picked up his guns from the ground and sprinted for the draw, bullets spurting dust around him.

"Is that son of a bitch hightailing it again?" Loretta said.

"Wouldn't surprise me none," Pike said.

The firing had died down and only a few shots were being exchanged. Pike thought he spotted Mexican Bob and Buff Kelly on the rim opposite him.

He glanced at the sky.

The sun was lower and shadows slanted among the trees. Black flies were already droning around McMullen's shattered head.

"Hey, you, Pike!"

"What do you want, Dredge?"

"Cut me loose and you and the woman are out of it."

"Go to hell."

"Pike, let bygones be bygones, I say. You put a bullet into me and I took your arm. We're even."

"We don't trust you, you pervert," Loretta said.

"I give you my word, missy. An' Clem Dredge's word is his bond." He paused, then: "Anybody will tell you that."

Loretta looked at Pike. "What do you think?"

"I don't believe a word he says."

"Me neither."

Loretta looked at the surrounding hills, at the drifts of smoke from rifle fire.

"We're all going to die," she said.

Minutes dragged past. Only a few sniping shots were fired and the gun battle was deteriorating into a standoff.

Dryden's men couldn't come down from the hills without exposing themselves to fire and the gunmen holed up in the trees were pinned down and couldn't move either.

Darkness would fall in a couple of hours with the coming of night and one side or the other could make its move.

Until then, Pike was prepared to wait.

But Henry Dryden changed all that.

He ran out of the draw, leading four saddled horses, immediately drawing fire.

"Charlie," he yelled, "where the hell are you?"

Pike rose. "Over here."

"Help me get Dredge on a horse."

Pike didn't move, thinking it through. Finally he decided that running was preferable to waiting.

Loretta at his heels, he sprinted to Dryden.

"Cut his feet loose and help me get him mounted," Dryden said.

A bullet ticked at the sleeve of Pike's gun arm as he kneeled beside Dredge and cut the rope from his ankles.

Dredge immediately kicked out at Pike, the heel of his boot hitting him hard on the thigh. Pike drew his gun and slammed the barrel into Dredge's head. The man groaned and fell back, his eyes rolling.

Pike and Dryden manhandled Dredge onto a horse, then mounted themselves. Loretta climbed onto the back of her paint and yelped as a bullet split the air close to her head.

"Lead the way, Charlie," Dryden said. "I'll take aholt of Dredge."

"Where the hell are we going?" Pike said.

"West, into the damned mountains." Dryden dug his heels into his horse. "Let's go."

Scattered shots followed them, probably fired by men on both sides. But now the shooting was wildly inaccurate, no one wanting to expose himself to draw a clear bead.

Taking the lead, Pike rode toward the humpbacked hill that rose steeply ahead of him. The slopes were covered with rocks and wind-twisted junipers and here and there the setting sun formed crouching shadows.

Beyond lay the mountains, majestic blue peaks outlined against a rose-colored sky, a sight to give a man pause and still the breath in his throat.

Up close, the hill was not as steep as it had seemed from a distance.

Pike led the way on the sure-footed dun, Loretta behind him, Dryden and the swaying, groaning Dredge taking up the rear.

Using a switchback game trail, Pike reached the crest and pulled his horse into the oaks. He swung out of the saddle and studied the land to the west.

The rise fell away gradually and opened into a wide, grassy valley. Arrow-shaped forests of oak and juniper thrust into the prairie land and ancient volcanic boulders, split by time and weather, stood watch like burly sentinels.

Beyond stretched serried ranks of hills, then mountains so high, they touched the face of God.

Pike stepped beside Dredge, who was bent over the saddle horn. He grabbed the man by the back of his shirt and let him fall to the ground.

"Let him sleep it off for a spell," he said to Dryden.

"We can't linger here, Charlie," Dryden said. "They're still too close."

Pike lifted his head, listening into the faded day.

"Shooting's stopped," he said.

He looked at Dryden and stretched out his hand. "Glass."

The judge reached into his saddlebags and passed Pike the telescope.

Pike moved down the hill a few yards until he had a clear view, then scanned the meadow.

Everyone was gone.

CHAPTER 52

Charlie Pike grinned as he handed Dryden the glass.

"Skedaddled, every last one of them," he said.

"Why?"

Pike's grin grew wider. "I'd say they found McMullen's horse and your money box."

He watched Loretta sit with her back against a tree and hitch up her skirts to her knees.

"How much money did you have in there, Henry?"

"Nearly eight thousand in paper money and gold," Dryden said. "My life savings, all I had in the world."

He stared at Dredge, who was in a sitting position, slowly shaking his head. "They'll come for him. Maybe we'll get the money back."

Pike built a cigarette, not looking at Dryden. "Men with eight thousand dollars to spend on whiskey and whores don't want to get killed in a mean-nothing gunfight."

"You mean they'll leave him, abandon Dredge?"

"That's what I think. They've probably elected a new leader by this time, so why take a bullet for Clem Dredge?"

"The others? My . . . I mean McMullen's men?"

"They're either in cahoots with Simpson and them or everybody agreed to call it quits and go their own ways."

"So my savings are gone?"

Pike lit his cigarette. "Looks like."

Suddenly Dryden looked old and tired.

"We will go back to the meadow and wait there for the Chinaman," he said.

"It's over, Dryden," Pike said. "It's time we were going our separate ways."

"No, not yet, Charlie. Wait until the Chinaman gets here."

"You don't need me any longer, Dryden."

"But I do. I can't handle this alone."

"What the hell are you talking about?" Pike said.

"Charlie, listen to me, Dredge can make us rich." Dryden put his hand on Pike's shoulder.

"Wait that long, Charlie, just long enough to get wealthy."

Loretta stepped beside Pike.

"Charlie, this man is trash and I hate his guts. I'd rather you rode out, but you deserve something for your arm and for the way he ruined your life. If he can make you rich, let him do it."

Dryden's face hardened. He had seemed old before; now he looked mean and dangerous.

"Once again, pearls of wisdom from the mouth of a two-dollar whore," he said. "Listen to her, Charlie."

"What does Dredge know?" Pike asked him.

"The Chinaman will tell us. And later we may have to travel far, along perilous trails, and I'll need you by my side."

Dryden's eyes moved beyond Pike. "Ah, the man we've just been discussing," he said.

Dredge's hands were still tied behind his back, but he'd struggled to his feet. He stood swaying, his face bloody, a shaggy, bearded giant who looked more animal than man in the turning light.

"I have nothing to tell you, Dryden," he said, his voice thick. "Pike is right, this is over. Let me go and we'll forget the beefs that lie between us."

Dryden's smile was icy. "That is quite impossible, Mr. Dredge."

"Damn you, it's over."

"No, it's not over. Not until you meet the Chinaman and answer his question."

"I'm a white man, Dryden."

"I can see that."

"You can't let a Chinaman torture a white man."

"Who said anything about torture, Mr. Dredge? Answer the Chinaman's question truthfully and you will feel no torment."

"But I don't know nothing!" Dredge roared.

"That," Dryden said, "remains to be seen."

His eyes moved from Dredge to Pike. "Well, Charlie, will you stay?"

"Dryden, I won't stand by and watch a man tortured."

"Because he's a white man?"

"Any man."

"There will be no torture," Dryden said. "There, does that make you feel better?"

"I'll stick until the Chinaman gets here."

"Excellent fellow! Now, let us move back to the meadow. It's such a singularly pleasant spot."

Helped by Dryden, Pike dragged the unburied dead into the trees and covered them as best they could in dirt and branches.

Pike was in a somber mood.

Against his will, he had agreed to stay, as though Dryden exerted some kind of strange hold over him.

Had he done it for money? The promise of riches?

That was part of it, he admitted to himself.

He could rebuild the ranch, make it a decent place to bring a wife and raise children. He needed his own woman, a gal who walked with her back straight and her head up, the kind who could look a man in the eye and feel his equal.

And part of it, and here he cussed his own stubbornness, was a desire to see this thing through to the end. He had sacrificed too much to walk away from it now.

And there was another reason, one that had come to him on the hill as he witnessed Dryden's arrogance and casual cruelty.

He badly wanted to kill the man.

CHAPTER 53

"Why does he keep doing that, Charlie?" Loretta said.

"He's looking for the Chinaman," Pike said.

"In the dark?"

"There's a moon."

Three days had passed since they'd again camped in the meadow.

Dryden, restless and wild eyed, spent most of his time on the hills, watching for Chang.

"He's crazy," Loretta said. "And he's getting worse."

"He's also dangerous, Loretta. I don't trust a madman."

Dredge was tied to an oak, bound hand and foot.

"Hey, Pike," the man said, "what does he expect me to tell him?"

"You've asked me that before," Pike said. "I guess where you buried your gold."

"What gold? An outlaw spends all his

money on whiskey and women and it never lasts more'n a few weeks. That's why we keep robbing banks."

"Dryden thinks you've got gold buried somewhere and he wants it."

"Do you?"

"I don't know. He says the Chinaman will get the answer."

Dredge laughed. "There's only one answer — I don't have any gold."

"Save yourself," Loretta said. "Tell me and Charlie where the gold is hidden."

"Lady, there is no damned gold and there never was."

"Do you believe him, Charlie?" Loretta asked.

"Hell, I don't know what to believe anymore," Pike said.

"I know what to believe, Charlie."

Dryden stepped out of the darkness into the firelight. "Mr. Dredge is correct, he has no gold. But he knows where gold is hidden."

"If I knew where gold was hidden, I'd have dug it up a long time ago," Dredge said.

Dryden smiled. "Who said it needed to be dug up? I didn't."

He stepped closer to Dredge. "Your lying tongue has tripped you."

"Hell, Dryden, that's what you do with gold you want to hide, you put it in the ground. Have you never heard of pirates and buried treasure? What else would you do with it?"

"I don't know, Mr. Dredge. You tell me."

"There is no gold, Dryden. Get that through your head."

Pike lit a cigarette and said: "If it wasn't Dredge, who hid the gold in the first place?"

"Do you want to answer that, Mr. Dredge?" Dryden said.

He waited, then: "No? Then I will." He looked at Pike. "It was hidden by Mr. Dredge's brother. We're talking a fortune, Charlie."

Dredge let out a guffaw of genuine amusement. "Hell, Frank never had more than two dollars in his pocket at a time. All the money he ever got, he spent. Frank never buried no gold."

"That's not the information I received," Dryden said. "Unfortunately, after I hanged him."

"You was told wrong," Dredge said.

"Frank Dredge robbed a Topeka and Santa Fe train in Raton Pass and took one hundred thousand dollars in gold and paper money from the Wells Fargo safe," Dryden said. "Do you deny that?"

"He robbed a Santa Fe train, yeah."

"And the money was never accounted for."

"Because there was none," Dredge said. "You know what Frank got from that train robbery? Three dollars and sixteen cents and a bunch of bananas."

"You're a liar, Dredge," Dryden said. "You helped your brother hide the money somewhere near Raton Pass in the New Mexico Territory. You know where it is and eventually you'll tell me."

Dredge shook his head and in a small, flat voice said: "A hundred thousand dollars. Hell, I would've dug that up years ago."

"Hear him, Charlie?" Dryden said. "Listen to the guilt in his every lying word."

Something that was stretched taut snapped inside Dryden.

He lashed out at Dredge with his boot, kicking him again and again in his unprotected face and head.

"Liar!" he screamed. Then, with every thudding kick: "Liar! Liar! Liar!"

Pike sprang to his feet and pushed Dryden away. "Damn it, man, you'll kill him!"

Suddenly Dryden's gun was in his hand.

"Don't you dare manhandle me, Charlie. You ever do that again, I swear to God I'll drop you."

Without another word, Dryden holstered his gun, then turned on his heel and walked back toward the hill, darkness closing around him.

Dredge's face was bloody, a broken nose spilling green snot and scarlet gore over his chin.

"He's hurting, but he'll live," Pike said.

"Henry's mad, Charlie," Loretta said. "He's insane."

Pike nodded. "I know. And I think Dredge is telling the truth that there is no gold and there never was."

"You'll never convince Henry of that."

"I think he already knows and it's eating at him," Pike said. "But he's bet everything he owns on one throw of the dice. If there's no hidden gold, he's ruined."

"Serves him right," Loretta said.

"Dryden was a respected judge, a pillar of the community. Now he's looking down the road, seeing himself as a worthless old man, living on handouts."

Pike glanced at the moon. It was bright and the land was awash in its pale glow.

"Western towns are full of poor, broken-down old-timers with nothing to do and all day to do it in. Nobody is glad at their coming or sad at their leaving and for the most part they're ignored. A man like Dryden

335

doesn't like to be ignored."

Pike smiled slightly. "As far as he's concerned, there has to be a fortune buried in the ground somewhere. It will bring with it respect and the kind of life he thinks he deserves. Without it, he's nothing, a nobody."

"Where do we go from here, Charlie?" Loretta asked. The moonlight made a halo of her blond hair.

"I've been studying on it and we're leaving. Now."

She pointed to Dredge. "What about him?"

"What about him?"

"Are we taking him with us?"

"He means nothing to me."

"He's a pervert, but I don't like the idea of leaving him to the Chinaman," Loretta said.

"He's got nothing to tell the Chinaman. I guess his dying will be a long time in coming."

Pike glanced at Dredge, who was groaning softly, his head twitching.

He remembered the man at the Mexican village, dragging the terrified girl back into the cantina. And how he casually shot the unarmed villager who came to her aid.

Everyone lives, not everybody deserves to.

Dredge was one of the latter.

But, no matter how he tried to harden himself, Pike's conscience would not allow the man to die the kind of death the Chinaman would give him.

"We'll take him with us," he said.

It was a decision he'd come to regret.

Chapter 54

"Seems like every time we put this man on a horse, he's unconscious," Pike said.

He and Loretta had managed to get Dredge more or less upright in the saddle, but the man was still out of it.

Moonlight lay on the far bank of the draw, shadow on the other. The zebra dun stamped its foot and snorted as Pike tightened the cinch.

Loretta was already mounted. She stared into the darkness.

"Where the hell is Henry?" she said.

"Still up on the hill, I hope," Pike said.

"I don't trust that crazy son of a bitch. He'd probably shoot us both."

"Probably," Pike said.

He put his foot in the stirrup.

Then Clem Dredge read to him from the book.

The outlaw drew back his leg and kicked Pike hard between the shoulders, the high heel of his boot slamming into the spine.

Pike went down, feeling as if he'd been hit by a twenty-pound sledgehammer.

Dredge's hands were tied behind him, but he kneed his horse around and galloped into the darkness.

The taste of green bile in his mouth, Pike lay facedown on the grass.

In the distance he heard a shot, then another.

"Charlie, are you all right?" Loretta said, kneeling beside him.

Pike struggled to draw a breath. "I'll be fine."

He got to his feet. "Let's get the hell out of here before Dryden starts shooting at us."

Pike climbed into the saddle. From the waist up, everything hurt, his back, the still-tender stump of his arm. His pride.

He had badly underestimated Dredge's toughness and the man's ability to take punishment. And he'd paid for it.

"You ready, Loretta?" he said.

"As I'll ever be."

"Then let's go."

They ran their horses toward the end of the meadow, where the hills dropped onto the flat.

"After him, Charlie! Find him!"

Dryden was loping down the slope, stiff-legged in his haste, waving Pike on.

Then they were into the rolling country, heading north toward the Rio Bravo.

Pike eased the dun into a walk and Loretta pulled alongside him.

"He thought we were helping him," she said. "Going after Dredge."

"Yeah, shows you how nuts he is."

"Where to, Charlie?"

"I'm heading for my ranch. You tagging along?"

Loretta shrugged. "I got nothing better to do at the moment."

"We should be there in three, four days."

"We've no grub."

"There are villages along the way."

"Well, let's hope we find one sooner rather than later," Loretta said. "All this excitement has me worn out."

Pike and Loretta rode into a village in the late afternoon of the next day, a collection of low adobes clustered around a central plaza.

A cantina, four timber posts supporting a straw roof, promised food and drink.

"*Dos* mescal," Loretta ordered at the bar.

She slugged her drink down and ordered another.

"What do you think, Charlie?" she said.

"Have we seen the last of Dryden?"

"Maybe."

"Dredge?"

"Maybe."

"You're a gold mine of information, ain't you?"

"Either one, or both, could come after us. I want to meet them on my home ground."

"Let's hope that pistolero Billy is always talking about — what's his name?"

"Pete Sanchez."

"Yeah, him. Let's hope he's back to home."

Pike nodded. "He's a good man with the Colt. Mighty sudden and sure."

"Better than Clem Dredge?"

"It would be a close-run thing."

"You seen Sanchez kill a man?"

"No. The only things I've seen him shoot are bean cans."

"Dredge is no bean can. Neither is Dryden."

"Sanchez has killed seven men."

"Who says?"

"Billy."

"Billy says. Billy says a lot of things."

She looked at the elderly *cantinero.* "Hey, pops, you got anything to eat?"

The man looked baffled.

"Eat." She made an eating motion with

her fingers. *"Comer."*

"Tortillas y pollo guisado, señorita." Then in English. "You like?"

"I like. We'll sit over there at the table."

"What are we having?" Pike asked after they sat.

"Tortillas and chicken stew. You like chicken stew?"

"No."

"Well, that's what we're having."

Pike scraped his first bowl down to the pottery and was working on a second when Loretta stretched out a hand and stilled his spoon.

"Charlie, for a man who doesn't like chicken stew, you sure like chicken stew."

Pike shrugged. "I don't like Billy's chicken stew. This is nothing like it." He smiled. "Studying on it, I don't like Billy's anything, except maybe his biscuits."

"You need a good woman, Charlie."

"Are you putting yourself up for the job, Loretta?"

"I'm not a good woman."

"You're all right."

"I'm a whore. I wouldn't be good for you."

Pike glanced at the *cantinero,* who either had not heard or did not understand.

"Don't whores retire sometime?" he said.

"Not this one. When I retire it'll be because I've started my own house. I don't want to marry, ever."

"Hell, Loretta, I wouldn't marry you anyway."

"Why?"

"Because you're a whore."

"So you're holding that against me?"

"But you just said —"

"You're too good to marry a whore. Is that it, Charlie?"

"But you said —"

"Now I know what kind of man you are, Charlie. A skunk."

"But —"

"I'll be fine in a minute, I assure you," Loretta said. She took a square of lace from her pocket and dabbed at her eyes.

"I've heard that kind of talk before from a man," she said, "but never put so crudely."

"Loretta, I didn't mean to —"

"I don't want to talk about it anymore, Charlie. You've said enough."

Pike felt as if Loretta had tied him in knots, then jumped on him.

He'd lost his appetite for the stew and pushed the bowl away from him.

After I while, he said: "I just meant —"

"I know what you meant."

Another pause, then: "Loretta, hell, I'd marry you."

"You're just saying that."

"No, I mean it."

Loretta sniffed. "Charlie Pike, I wouldn't marry you if you were the last man on earth. Besides, I'm a whore."

Rather than step into the same bear trap twice, Pike built a smoke and kept his mouth shut.

There was no hotel in the village, but the old cantina owner let Pike and Loretta spread their blankets on the dirt floor of his modest establishment.

In the morning, Loretta icily polite, he served them a breakfast of tortillas and more chicken stew.

Before they left, the old man filled a sack with tortillas, dried goat meat and a bottle of mescal.

Pike gave the *cantinero* the last of his money; then he and Loretta took to the trail again.

Three days later they rode into Pike's ranch.

CHAPTER 55

During the next weeks, Pike and Billy Childes divided their time between rebuilding the cabin and checking on the herd.

The longhorns were scattered, some of them as far north as the plateau breaks and its high, flower-covered meadows. The cattle seemed to be faring well and had put on weight.

A neighboring rancher put on a cotillion to celebrate the arrival of his new Hereford bull. Pike was impressed by the animal, but decided to reserve judgment until after the winter freeze.

Maxine showed up, complained about her husband, then, discouraged by Loretta's presence, left.

Loretta buried her nose in *The Fair Maid of Perth,* after accusing Pike of "burning poor Sir Walter Scott to a crisp."

She ousted Pike and Billy from the bunkhouse and forced them to spread their blankets outside. She also insisted that the outhouse be rebuilt before the cabin. This time Pike settled for a one-holer, but only as a temporary measure, hinting that an unheard-of three-holer might well be his next masterwork.

To Billy's joy, Loretta took over the cooking and Pike was forced to admit that, even with her limited culinary skills, the resulting meals were a great improvement.

Billy was stung by a scorpion hiding out in the lumber and, for a day, was too sick to work. Loretta fussed over him the whole time and Pike suspected that was the reason Billy pretended to be so poorly.

A reverend from town, an earnest young man with a constantly dripping nose, stopped by.

When Loretta told him about her profession, she and the reverend sang "I Saw the Light," and then Loretta invited him to stay to supper.

The long summer days rolled past and Pike, thanks to good food and plenty of rest, grew stronger. The pain in the stump of his left arm all but disappeared and Billy reckoned he'd put on twenty pounds.

Time is a great healer and gradually Pike pushed Clem Dredge and Henry Dryden to the back of his mind.

But they were always there, like night riders over the horizon, an ominous threat that would eventually come his way.

Then came the day in late summer when he was forced to confront the realization that the time had come.

That morning Billy took him aside after breakfast and said: "He was there again last night, boss. Up on the hill."

"Hell, Billy, why didn't you tell me?" Pike said.

"What good would it have done? You head toward him and he disappears."

Pike was silent and Billy said: "You figure it's ol' Hangin' Hank?"

"Maybe. Or Clem Dredge."

"If I had my druthers, I'd prefer Hank."

"Don't underestimate him, Billy. He's good with a gun, maybe better than Dredge."

"What do they want from us, boss?"

"Dryden, I don't rightly know. Unless it's to get even with Loretta and me for running out on him."

"Clem?"

"I put a bullet into him and handled him pretty rough."

"Throwing him out a window was rough. You're right about that."

"So was bending the barrel of a Colt over his thick skull."

"You think he plans to even the score?"

"Could be. He ain't a man to kiss and make up."

Billy thought for a few moments, then shook his head. "Nah, boss, it don't figure. I bet ol' Clem has forgot all about you an' he's hiding out in Mexico someplace."

"You think so?"

"I'm sure so. Clem Dredge ain't gonna bother hisself getting even with you."

Billy grinned. "Getting buffaloed and tossed out a window is nothing to him. Hell, worse has happened to him on a drunk."

"What are you two talking about?" Loretta said.

She stepped beside the men. "Are you plotting something? About shirking your chores, maybe?"

"The rider was up on the hill again last night," Pike said.

"Henry?"

"I don't know. Could be."

"Or Clem Dredge?" Loretta said.

"I was just telling the boss that ol' Clem ain't gonna bother us," Billy said. "Hell, we're only pissant cattlemen. We don't drive the train or blow the whistle."

Loretta was quiet for a long time. An

uneasy, distant-eyed quiet.

Finally she said: "They won't let it go, Charlie. Neither of them."

Pike had heard something he already knew. He said: "You reckon, huh?"

"Henry won't let it go because he's obsessed and completely mad. Dredge because he's the devil's spawn and never forgets a slight."

Pike smiled. "Maybe you rate Dredge too highly."

"I don't underestimate him."

Pike's eyes moved to the hill where the wind stirred the live oaks and juniper and set the scrub jays to quarreling.

"One of them will come soon," he said.

"Well, let's hope it's Hangin' Hank an' not Clem," Billy said.

"Either way," Loretta said, "I see troubles coming down."

Two days passed and the rider was no longer seen on the hill.

But on the night of the third day, the voice called out from among the dark oaks.

"Charlie Pike . . ."

His name was long drawn out, an eerie sound in the darkness.

Pike rose from his blankets and stood, listening.

"Charlie Pike . . ."

Billy was beside him, then Loretta, wearing only her shift.

"Get your coffin ready, Charlie. . . ."

"Where is it coming from?" Loretta said.

Nobody answered her.

"Dig the hole deep, Charlie . . . down where the worms crawl. . . ."

"Is it Dredge?" Billy said. "Damn him, is it Dredge?"

"I'm coming for you, Charlie. . . ."

A pause, then: "Gonna kill you, boy. . . ."

"It's a ghost," Loretta said.

"The worms will be eatin' you soon, Charlie. . . ."

Billy took a couple of steps forward.

"Let's see if a ghost can take a bellyful of forty-fives," he said.

His Colt came up and he blasted five quick shots at the crest of the hill.

Their echoes were still racketing through the restless dark as derisive peals of laughter broke from the brush like a flock of night birds.

"You'll have to do better than that when I come for you, Charlie. . . ."

"Leave it, Billy, no more," Pike said. "He's trying to scare us."

"He's succeeding," Loretta said. "He's scaring the hell out of me."

Pike cupped his hand to his mouth.

"Dredge, you son of a bitch, come down and face me like a man."

"Soon, Charlie . . . real soon. . . ."

Silence again claimed the night.

Billy, as though he could not stand the sudden quiet, said: "He'll come at us straight up. We'll be ready for him."

"I told you before, Billy, it's not your fight," Pike said,

"An' I told you before, I ride for the brand."

"Then so be it. And thank you, Billy. Thank you kindly."

Pike turned to Loretta. "If we fall, and that's highly likely, you'll suffer worse than any of us. I wouldn't blame you none if you rode out."

"I'll study on it, Charlie," Loretta said. "Whatever I decide, you'll be the first to know."

Out in the hills, secure in their gloomy fastness, the gray coyotes gave voice to the moon, complaining of their hunger.

Three days later Clem Dredge came for Charlie Pike and Loretta still hadn't made up her mind.

CHAPTER 56

Clem Dredge walked out of a fine bright morning, the kind that makes a man want to hold on to the day he has and wish for no other.

Sunlight burnished the land to the sheen of new brass and the wind that stirred the trees whispered a promise of autumn, its breath as cool as frost.

Dredge dismounted at a distance and walked toward the ranch house. Pike watched him come.

He left the saw he'd been using in the timber and strapped on his gun belt.

The moment had arrived and Pike felt little emotion.

"Let's get it over with, Dredge," he called out.

The man smiled. "That's why I'm here, Charlie."

Dredge stopped a few yards away. He wore a bone-handled Colt with a seven-and-a-half-inch barrel, Texas style. His eyes were shaded by his hat brim, his beard and long hair tangled with sunlight.

After looking beyond the outlaw, Pike focused on him again and said: "Where are your boys?"

"All dead, Charlie."

"Dryden's men?"

"Hell no. Dryden's bunch couldn't take my boys."

Dredge's smile stretched into a grin. "I killed them my own self."

"That was white of you, Dredge. Save the law a job."

"They were thieves, fornicators, gamblers and drunks and I gunned them one by one."

Dredge shook his head. "Well, all but a no-account named Jacob Milner. Last I saw of him he was running into the desert on bare feet, holding up his drawers. I didn't kill him because he made me laugh." He shrugged. "If we meet again and he don't make me laugh, I'll kill him then."

The man's grin faded, vanished. "Anyhoo, they all learned that nobody runs out on Clem Dredge. Nobody."

"J. M. Simpson was no pushover. I guess you shot him in the back, Dredge. Seems like your style."

The man would not let himself be prodded.

"He wasn't much. I took him in a saloon in Brackettville."

Dredge smiled again. "Ol' Johnny boy got my bullet in his belly an' he chawed up the floor so much, I reckon he's still tasting sawdust in hell."

"Boss! I'm on your left," Billy said suddenly.

"And I'm on your right with a Winchester," Loretta said.

Without turning, Pike said: "Light out of here now, Loretta."

"I ride for the brand, Charlie."

There was little time to explore the emotion, but Pike was touched.

But now he was scared, for himself and even more for Loretta and Billy.

Dredge grinned and shook his head. "You got your hired hand protecting you, Charlie, and a woman's skirts to hide behind."

He flexed the fingers of his gun hand. "What the hell am I going to do with you?"

"You're gonna shut your big trap and haul iron."

"Ah, the very thing," Dredge said.

He went for his gun.

Dredge had taken time to calculate the

order and it showed.

Pike first, since he believed he was the fastest.

Then Billy.

Then the woman.

But he wanted her alive or wounded just enough to enjoy her for a few hours.

He had miscalculated badly.

No one had underestimated Dredge. But he had underestimated Billy. He had dismissed a tough-as-nails cowboy with sand as a second-rater. And that was a serious mistake.

Dredge's gun came up fast and he fired at Pike.

Pike took the hit and fired wild.

But then Dredge staggered, hit square by Billy's bullet.

He roared his rage and fired at Billy.

Then Dredge groaned loudly as a shot fired from Loretta's Winchester thudded into his side.

Pike, angry with himself for missing so badly, fired again. This time his aim was true and he hit Dredge high in the chest.

The outlaw went to his knees, blood on his lips.

Dredge snarled and tried to bring up his Colt again.

Pike, Billy and Loretta fired at almost the

same time.

Shredded by bullets, Dredge screamed and fell on his side. He was out of it and the fight was over.

Pike looked at Billy. The young cowboy's left arm hung limp at his side, his shoulder blossoming scarlet.

Loretta seemed unhurt, though her face was pale, her lips bloodless.

Dredge's bullet had torn into Pike's thigh and now the pain had taken a hold of him and was punishing him considerably.

He limped to Dredge and used his foot to turn the man on his back.

Dredge was still alive, but barely.

"Damned cowboy fooled me," he said. "He was quick."

"Seems like," Pike said.

"Hey, Charlie, come closer."

Pain slammed through Dredge and he arched his back against the spasm.

For a moment, Pike thought he was gone, but the man spoke again, gasping.

"Tell . . . tell Dryden the money is buried where he'll never find it. Tell him there's so many double eagles, a man couldn't spend them all in two lifetimes."

"Where is it?" Pike asked. He told himself it was curiosity, not greed.

"Wouldn't you like to know?" Dredge

grinned.

And died.

Loretta stepped beside Pike. "Let me see it," she said.

Pike extended his left leg. "I'm bleeding like a pig."

After she kneeled and took a look, Loretta rose to her feet. "The bullet went right through. I don't think it hit the bone."

"If I lost my leg, I'd be exactly half a man," Pike said. He smiled.

"It's not funny, Charlie," Loretta said. "Don't make jokes about that."

She stared at Billy. "Come here, you."

"It's nothing, Loretta," Billy said.

"Bullshit. Come here."

Loretta examined the wound in Billy's shoulder. "Dredge's bullet is still in there. It's got to come out."

Billy looked at her with puppy dog eyes. "It pains me considerable, Loretta."

"I'm sure it does."

"All over the shoulder and into my back," Billy said.

"You're a poor, wounded thing, Billy," Loretta said. She kissed him on the cheek.

"Tell me that again, Loretta," Billy said.

Loretta smiled, then looked at Pike. "I'll hitch up the wagon. I'm taking you into

357

town. You both need a doctor."

"I'll help you," Pike said.

"No, you won't. The bleeding in your leg has stopped, I don't want it to start all over again."

She glanced at Dredge. "Is he dead?"

"As he'll ever be. Said he didn't account for Billy." Pike grinned. "He didn't account for you either."

"I'll hitch up the wagon," Loretta said. "Don't go anywhere until I'm done."

"Ain't likely, the way I'm hurting," Pike said.

"You're a poor, wounded thing, Charlie," Loretta said. "There, feel all better now?"

"Where's the kiss?"

"You don't get one."

"Why?"

"Because you're too damn mean, Charlie."

CHAPTER 57

Dr. Joachim von Bock was a tall, thin man with piercing green eyes and the bedside manner of a hungover cougar.

He examined Billy, then Pike.

After hurriedly binding up Pike's leg, he said: "You can stay here in the waiting room for now. I must operate on your *kamerad* immediately."

"How is he?" Loretta said.

"The bullet is deep, *fraulein*."

"Hey, Doc, have you done this before?" Pike asked. "I mean with the bullet being so deep an' all?"

"A hundred times. A thousand. I've lost count."

"Were you in the war, Doc?"

"Which war?"

"The War Between the States, of course."

"No. I was an officer in the Prussian army during the late war against the French. I had the honor to be commanded by Crown

Prince Friedrich Wilhelm and received the Iron Cross from his own hands."

"Fair piece off your home range."

"Yes."

Pike didn't push it.

Men headed west for reasons of their own. Some shared the why of it, others didn't.

"You will assist me, *fraulein,*" von Bock said. "There is a clean apron hanging in the surgery."

Loretta looked as though she was about to snap to attention.

She didn't, settling for "I'd love to, Doctor."

Billy looked like a puppy dog again. "Will you hold my hand, Loretta?"

"No, she will not hold your hand," von Bock snapped. "You will be tough, Herr Childes, tough as Krupp's steel."

He glared at Loretta. "Take him into surgery. We will proceed at once."

Pike found another chair to prop up his aching leg, picked up the local paper and lost himself in the doings of Placerville.

A woman named Pickens had discharged a scattergun at a fox in her henhouse. She'd hit her old man instead and Dr. von Bock had removed eighteen buckshot from the man's ass. He was expected to survive.

Some rooster who called himself Wild Dog Dugan got drunk and proceeded to take pots at a hardware store sign. He was thrown in the local slammer to sober up.

A straight-backed chair was reported missing from a residential porch on Second Street and thievery was suspected.

There were more stray dogs in town than ever before and the newspaper's editorial urged that local lawmen start performing their duties for a change and shoot them on sight.

Pike closed his eyes and his head drooped as sleep took him.

He dreamed of Clem Dredge.

An hour ticked past. . . .

The door of the waiting room opened and Pike was instantly awake. He was about to ask after Billy, but the look on Loretta's face stopped him.

She sat on a chair and buried her face in her hands, her slender shoulders shaking.

Pike struggled to his feet. "Loretta, what happened?"

It took a few long moments before Loretta looked at him from tearstained eyes.

"Billy is dead," she said.

Words tangled in Pike's throat, but his stunned face asked the question that Loretta now answered.

"His heart was weak. It . . . it just stopped."

"The doctor," Pike said. "How did he . . . how . . ."

"The doctor did his best to save him, Charlie."

"But . . . Billy was strong, Loretta."

"Yes, he was a strong little man. But he had a weak pump. Born with it, the doc says."

Pike went back to his chair and sat, his eyes staring into nothing.

Then Dr. von Bock was standing beside him.

"I'm sorry, Mr. Pike. I did all I could. The bullet was deep and his heart could not take the strain."

Pike wanted to lash out, blame the doctor, blame God . . . blame himself.

But he did not. He sat in silence.

"Now I must treat your leg," von Bock said. "And I want to take a look at the stump of your arm."

"Damn you, Billy is lying dead back there!" Pike said.

"Yes, and now my concern is with the living."

Pike was furious, almost blinded by his anger. "How can you be so damned calm? You just killed a man."

Von Bock's expression did not change. "I have seen many deaths, some of them terrible. If I died a little with each one, I would be unable to continue as a physician."

"Charlie, if you want to blame someone, blame me," Loretta said. "I was there when it happened."

Pike was quiet for a long time, his eyes fixed on a spot across the room.

Finally he said: "Billy is gone. It's done. Over. Blaming someone now is as unfair as it is pointless."

He looked at von Bock. "My leg hurts like hell, Doc."

"*Fraulein,* if the wounds show any sign of gangrene, color, smell, you will bring Herr Pike to me at once," von Bock said. "Do you understand?"

"Yes, Doctor."

Von Bock looked at Pike. "Your arm was amputated by a skilled surgeon. Was it in the war?"

"No. It was taken off in Mexico by a former soldier."

"An ex–medical officer?"

"No. I think he was an infantryman."

"He did well."

Von Bock laid a hand on Pike's shoulder. "I can arrange to have your *kamerad* buried here in town."

"No, we'll take him home with us. I want to bury him in his own soil."

"That would be your ranch?"

"Yes. Billy rode for the brand."

CHAPTER 58

That evening, just as the light was changing, Pike and Loretta buried Billy Childes on the range.

Pike had fashioned a cross from the timber he had bought to rebuild the cabin and he and Loretta placed it upright on the grave. Pike said all the words from the Good Book he could remember, then a few of his own.

Afterward Loretta sang "I'll Take You Home Again Kathleen," and it was done.

Pike mounted his horse and Loretta handed him the end of the rope that had been tied around Clem Dredge's ankles.

He dragged the body well away from Billy's grave and into a pile of limestone rock, then tossed the rope on top of it.

"A wooden cross on top of a hill in the middle of a wilderness don't signify," Pike said when he rejoined Loretta. "It says nothing about a man or his life."

"At the end, that's all Jesus had," Loretta said.

Pike stared at her. "You reckon that was enough for him?"

"It was enough."

She mounted her paint. "Charlie, as long as we're alive, Billy will be remembered," she said. "We'll say his name now and again."

Pike nodded. "I'll come here and talk to him."

"He'll like that."

"Yeah, he will. He was surely a talking man."

Over the next couple of days, Pike's leg showed signs of healing well and it no longer pained him as badly.

He continued his work on the cabin and Loretta helped him. On the afternoon of the third day, they were able to move inside, a slab of rock for a table and blankets on the floor for beds.

That same day Henry Dryden showed up, the Chinaman with him.

Pike met him outside with a gun on his hip and hatred in his eye.

"Nice to see you again, Charlie," Dryden said.

"The feeling ain't mutual," Pike said.

Dryden smiled and made to step down, but Pike's voice stopped him.

"Just set where you're at, Dryden," he said. "You're not welcome here."

Dryden's face hardened. "Don't push it, Charlie."

"I'm pushing it," Pike said. "I want you off my place."

He was aware of Loretta stepping beside him, a rifle in her hands.

"You ran out on me, Charlie, like the yellow dog you are," Dryden said.

"Best thing I ever done. I just wish to hell I'd done it earlier."

Dryden sat back in the saddle. "All I can expect here is abuse and impertinence, so I'll cut to the chase: Where is Clem Dredge?"

"He's dead."

Dryden looked as if he'd been slapped. "What do you mean, he's dead?"

"I mean he ain't breathing any longer."

"Who killed him?"

"I did. Or we did, Loretta, Billy Childes and me. Dryden killed Billy and put a bullet into me."

"The treasure! Did he say anything about the treasure?"

"Yes."

Dryden looked to be on the verge of hysteria. "Tell me, damn you! Tell me what he said."

"He told me it's buried where you'll never find it," Pike said, enjoying this. "More money than a man could spend in two lifetimes."

"He told you! He told you where the gold is hidden?"

He waved a hand. "The Chinaman will get it out of you. Damn your eyes, he'll cut it out of you."

"I asked Dredge, but he wouldn't tell me," Pike said, smiling.

"You're a damned liar."

"He's telling the truth, Henry," Loretta said, ice in her voice. "He wouldn't tell Charlie where it is."

Pike said: "But he was real particular that I should let you know that there was buried gold, Dryden."

Dryden had been a jurist long enough to tell when a man was holding back the truth. He could detect no lie in Pike.

Neither could the Chinaman.

Without a word, his face empty, the little man swung his mule around and rode away. There was no work for him here.

Dryden's shoulders slumped. He looked old and very tired.

"Then it's over," he said. "All this for nothing."

"That's right, Henry," Pike said. "Billy Childes' death, my arm, my ranch burned to the ground, all for nothing."

"That's not important," Dryden said.

"Then what is, Henry?"

"That I've lost my money. All I had, all I planned on having, gone."

"My heart breaks for you, Henry," Loretta said.

"New York, London, Paris . . . the life of a wealthy gentleman, my dreams, vanished."

He stared at Pike. "You know what it's like for a man to lose all his dreams?"

"Yeah," Pike said, "it's right behind me."

Dryden shook his head and his eyes glazed. He was looking down a long trail that offered him nothing. "I'll be a broken old man living on charity. I'll be a nonentity, a nobody with no respect from men, ignored by beautiful women."

"You told us you were dying, Henry," Pike said. "Better for you if your lie had been the truth."

"Nothing . . ." Dryden swung his horse away. "I have nothing. . . ."

Three days later, the west wind brought the smell of rot, decay, putrefaction . . . the stench of death.

CHAPTER 59

Henry Dryden had hanged himself from the limb of a cottonwood.

Pike and Loretta found him a mile west of the ranch, in a pleasant, shady gulch with a running stream and abundant ferns and wild oaks.

Dryden, an expert hangman, had left slack in the rope, hoping to break his neck after he quirted his horse out from under him.

He had not succeeded.

His toes were only inches from the ground and he had died hard, mouth agape, tongue lolling, eyes bugging out of his head.

As many suicides do, he had stripped naked and the coyotes had been busy on him, shredding his lower legs to the green bone.

Loretta held her handkerchief to her nose and mouth.

"Stinks, doesn't he?" she said, her words muffled.

"He stank worse when he was alive," Pike said.

He reached up and cut the rope. Dryden's body thudded to the ground.

"I want his guns," Loretta said.

"He's got no use for them," Pike said.

Loretta picked up Dryden's Colt and rifle and Pike said: "Why do you want those?"

"I have a use for them, Charlie."

"What use?"

"You'll see."

"When?"

"Soon, Charlie. When I'm ready."

"Then I won't push it."

"Not now. I'll tell you when."

A sheet of paper lying on top of Dryden's clothes caught Loretta's attention. She picked it up and gave it a quick glance.

"He left a note," she said. "It's for you, Charlie. You want to read it?"

"Let me have it," Pike said.

He took the note from Loretta and, without looking at it, tore it into shreds and dropped them on the ground.

"I wish I'd done that with the first one he sent me," he said.

Loretta glanced at Dryden's grotesque body.

"You want to say anything, Charlie?"

"No. Do you?"

Loretta shrugged. "Rest in peace, Henry."

She gathered up the reins of her horse. "Now let's get the hell out of here."

On a morning three weeks later, Pike was drinking coffee, smoking his first cigarette of the day, when Loretta led her saddled horse from the corral.

"Riding early," Pike said.

"I'm leaving, Charlie."

"Leaving? For where?"

Loretta opened her purse and showed Pike a key. "Henry left me his house, remember? I'm going back to claim it."

Pike was stunned. "Loretta, you can't do that, a woman alone riding all that way. There are bandits, Apaches, God knows what else."

"I've got a rifle and a revolver, Charlie. I'll be all right."

"But I like having you here. Hell, you haven't even finished *The Fair Maid of Perth* yet."

"I'm taking her with me, Charlie."

"But . . . but I want you to stay with me, Loretta. I'll marry you if you want that."

Loretta smiled and shook her head. "I'm not a wife, Charlie. I'm a whore. That's what I do best. I can't turn my back on it now and piss on my life."

The cigarette burned away between Pike's fingers and he yelped and shook his hand.

"Hell, Loretta, I need you here."

Loretta swung into the saddle and hiked her skirts above her knees.

"So long, Charlie. Sanchez will be back soon and you'll do just fine."

She swung her horse away, heading north.

"Hey, Loretta," Pike called out.

Loretta turned her head. "What is it, Charlie?"

"How come we never, you know, did it together?"

"Because you never paid me, Charlie."

The silver echoes of Loretta's laughter lingered long after she was gone.

And suddenly Charlie Pike felt lonelier than he'd ever been in his life.

ABOUT THE AUTHOR

Ralph Compton stood six foot eight without his boots. He worked as a musician, a radio announcer, a songwriter, and a newspaper columnist. His first novel, *The Goodnight Trail,* was a finalist for the Western Writers of America Medicine Pipe Bearer Award for Best Debut Novel. He was also the author of the *Sundown Riders* series and the *Border Empire* series.